ROUTLEDGE LIBRARY EDITIONS:
ARTHURIAN LITERATURE

Volume 5

MERLIN AND LEGENDARY ROMANCE

MERLIN AND LEGENDARY ROMANCE

CAROL E. HARDING

LONDON AND NEW YORK

First published in 1988

This edition first published in 2015
by Routledge
2 Park Square, Milton Park, Abingdon, Oxfordshire OX14 4RN

and by Routledge
711 Third Avenue, New York, NY 10017

Routledge is an imprint of the Taylor and Francis Group, an informa business

First issued in paperback 2015

British Library Cataloguing in Publication Data
A catalogue record for this book is available from the British Library

ISBN 978-1-138-02487-8 (Set)
eISBN 978-1-315-76522-8 (Set)
ISBN 978-1-138-78541-0 (hbk) (Volume 5)
ISBN 978-1-138-99579-6 (pbk) (Volume 5)
ISBN 978-1-315-76527-3 (ebk) (Volume 5)

Publisher's Note
The publisher has gone to great lengths to ensure the quality of this book but points out that some imperfections from the original may be apparent.

Disclaimer
The publisher has made every effort to trace copyright holders and would welcome correspondence from those they have been unable to trace.

CAROL E. HARDING

MERLIN AND LEGENDARY ROMANCE

GARLAND PUBLISHING, INC.
NEW YORK & LONDON
1988

Library of Congress Cataloging–in–Publication Data

Harding, Carol E., 1953–
Merlin and legendary romance.

(Garland publications in comparative literature)
Abstract of thesis (Ph.D.)—Indiana University, 1985.
Bibliography: p.
1. Merlin (Legendary character)—Romances—History and criticism. 2. Literature, Medieval—Themes, motives. 3. Arthurian romances—History and criticism. I. Title. II. Series.
PN57.M4H37 1988 809'.93351 88–21164
ISBN 0–8240–7488–2

The volumes in this series are printed on acid–free, 250–year–life paper.

Printed in the United States of America

In Memoriam

Herman J. Deutsch

Homo Probitatis

TABLE OF CONTENTS

Merlin prophesies to Vortigern (Huth) (British Museum Add. Ms. 38117, f. 38v)
Reproduced by permission of the British Library

Merlin disguised as a peasant (Vulgate) (British Museum Add. Ms. 10292, f. 129r)

Merlin arranges Arthur's marriage (Huth) (British Museum Add. Ms. 38117, f. 147r)
Reproduced by permission of the British Library

Merlin arranges Arthur's marriage (Huth) (British Museum Add. Ms. 38117, f. 147r)
Reproduced by permission of the British Library

Introduction

Ever since he was imprisoned by his lover in thirteenth-century France, Merlin has been revived by a succession of authors. Ranging from cameo appearances in Ariosto, Cervantes and C. S. Lewis to extended treatments in Tennyson, T. H. White and Mary Stewart, the enigma of Merlin defies permanent burial. In the honored tradition of medieval composition, the _matiere_ of the legend of Merlin has been reworked time and again to create a new _sens_.

But what was the old _sens_, the _sens_ of those thirteenth-century romances which codified the legend? This matter remains unresolved. For years, critics have passed over the Merlin texts and gone directly to the more popular sections on the Grail Quest and the Arthurian apocalypse. While the _Merlins_ have been recognized as part of the larger cycles, critics have treated them as less-than-intrinsic elements, even dismissing them as late additions which add nothing but plot background. While this study cannot seek to reverse all the misdirection of prior scholarship, it does attempt to remove some of the critical soil which has been tossed on Merlin's tomb.

Taking up the topic of Merlin, or indeed any Arthurian topic, opens the writer to such a vast pool of resources that even the first step may well qualify as masochistic. Still, it is possible to restrict the field of investigation. While such narrowing takes the risk of reaching conclusions of limited validity, it is the only workable course. The restrictions I have reached confine my inquiry to Merlin's role within two major medieval romances, the Vulgate _Merlin_ and Huth _Merlin_, but to put the French romances into some perspective, I also consider several earlier and one later text. Yet even in choosing the Merlin romances, I have had to leave aside their surrounding cycles and should explain my rationale.

The French _Merlins_ contain the fullest expression of Merlin as a character in medieval literature. While other texts present Merlin among the cast, either such works derive from these romances, or Merlin plays a very minor role. I dismiss none of these works as irrelevant, but believe the conclusions reached concerning the figure in the French _Merlins_ are transferable to the other works with little adjustment. The discussion of prior texts must, to some extent, stand alone, but their influence on the outlines of Merlin's figure and function is undeniable.

The cycles which contain the two Merlin texts, known as the Vulgate and the Pseudo-Robert de Boron or Post-Vulgate, are each several folio volumes in length. Dealing with both as a whole would prove unwieldy in this format. Merlin's presence in the other volumes is minimal, although his influence on events is evident. Again, the conclusions reached by concentrating on the _Merlin_ texts alone, I believe, sufficiently point the way to further application, as I tentatively indicate where appropriate.

Two problems must be addressed before discussing the works themselves. The first concerns genre, as the _Merlin_ texts do not fit typical romance definitions. The second concerns the place of fantasy or the marvellous--I shall use these terms interchangeably[1] --within the genre, which needs discussing since attitudes towards this technique have changed over the past decade or two.

Entire books have been written on romance, and on medieval romance, so without pretending thoroughness, I will begin by providing a basic picture of the romance in the middle ages. Although two distinct ways of approaching romance have evolved, the multitemporal and the strictly medieval, I find the latter more useful since it focuses on the problems of a specific era. Represented by such distinguished scholars as Northrop Frye and John Stevens, the multitemporal method presents problems for medieval romance, as indeed Frye himself admits (Secular Scripture 4). Stevens, in following Frye's classifications, must center his discussion around themes and motifs within romances, and finds it difficult to focus on the genre as a whole; and we find little commentary dealing with the historical development of romance or with relationships between individual works.

The historical approach conceives of romance as a genre developing in the twelfth century and receding by the sixteenth. The romance has specific roots in medieval epic, and the later forms of romance (Renaissance and beyond) adapt the viable elements in the genre. This approach has been denigrated because its proponents earlier in the twentieth century, W.P. Ker and Erich Auerbach especially, expressed a condescending antipathy towards romance, perceiving it as degenerate epic. However much I disagree with this antipathy, I still find their time-delimited approach more potentially enlightening with regard to the texts I have chosen.

Critics have generally used the works of Chrétien de Troyes to categorize the medieval romance genre. Motifs and conventions drawn from these texts include the setting in a feudal society, in which the rules of chivalry are more or less dominant as a code for men's behavior; adventure as the mainstay for plot development; a predominant interest in the individual, or in the individual's relationship with society; the role of marvels in the work, ranging from the totally mysterious to the magical and miraculous; love directly affecting the narrative; and a sense of an evil Other, internal or external, to be conquered. Few theorists point to only one predominant trait that announces, "This is Romance." Beer explicitly says, "There is no single characteristic which distinguishes the romance from other literary kinds nor will every one of the characteristics . . . be present in each work that we would call a romance" (10). Hanning, however, in his study of twelfth-century romance, describes it as a genre of "becoming" (<u>Individual</u> 139), and Frye and Stevens, in describing romance in general, pick out the key of Idealism or non-realistic methodology (Frye, <u>Secular Scripture</u> 38; Stevens 20, 227).

Medieval romance shares the multifaceted definition of form with its non-contemporary parallels, but the problems of medieval romance are more closely connected with its development from epic forms, while later romance criticism must consider the post-Enlightenment development of realistic narratives. Scholes and

Kellogg in The Nature of Narrative delineate one version of the progress from epic: epic "dissolves" into two distinct forms, history on the one hand, and fiction or romance on the other, which were united under the epic classification (58). N. E. Griffin, too, sees a direct development from the epic into romance, ancient and medieval. He picks out credibility as the key, in which we can see an implied bias toward epic typical of his generation: "By a romance we commonly mean a tale of an improbable or, better, of an incredible character" which differs from epic, "which was once . . . a credible tale" (55). He further argues that the epic of one culture will, when transplanted and re-interpreted, become the romance of another (58).

In his famous chapter on epic and romance in The Making of the Middle Ages, R. W. Southern reveals similar theories, specifically commenting on changes noted from Roland to Chrétien's works, and in contrast to the literary scholars tends to exhibit a more descriptive than prescriptive attitude. Southern sees, for example, that the enemy in Roland is clearly defined, an outside enemy threatening the community. (Ganelon, having become a traitor, is "outside" in a different sense than the pagans, except that both have forfeited God's favor.) In Chrétien, the enemy is often unseen, mysterious, or even living within the knight himself as a kind of alter-ego, and the threat is more often against individuals than the community at large (244). More recently, Jameson indicated this change indirectly when he notes a conflict between an old view of evil, in which the enemy is permanently black (as in

Roland), and a new concept in which the enemy can cease to be evil (an unknown knight may be revealed as a friend). In this latter case, the evil in a text will tend to be placed outside human control since it cannot be permanently placed in one person or army (161).

The problem with classifying the Arthurian cycles arises both from the idea of progression from one genre to another, and from the nebulous definitions that have been presented. Because of critics' frustration with classifying this genre, they often go to great lengths to create a single genre, separate from epic and chanson de geste and lyric, which only leaves us with unique monsters belonging to "none of the above." Like the Arthurian cycles. Jameson (150) notes that the problem with most genre criticism is its use of arbitrary, oversimplified categories, as if critics were trying to adapt the scientific classification systems of genus and species to literature (153), and it just will not work. E. D. Hirsch makes a similar observation: "The one thing [about classification of literary genres] that does matter is the degree of reliance we place in the definitive character of these arbitrary schemata. If we believe they are constitutive rather than arbitrary and heuristic, then we have made a serious mistake and have also set up a barrier to valid interpretation" (111).

Scholes and Kellogg describe the Arthurian cycles as "epic romanticized" (208);[2] Beer notes that they thrive "in the shifting borderland between legend and fact" (22). Generations of Malory scholars have been equally frustrated in trying to classify Le Morte

Darthur. The problem lies in insisting upon clean boundaries. Like human beings themselves, literature possesses gray areas. One approach to dealing with the gray is that of Frye's *Anatomy* which discusses qualities rather than forms. Another would incorporate Hirsch's concept of a continuum, a line which intersects other lines, as romance intersects the lines of epic, of saint's life, of fantasy, and so forth.

> The broad genre is a loose family group. Many of the resemblances borne by members of the group have arisen by historical assimilation, while others are due entirely to the exigencies of thought and reality. The members are grouped together as a class for conceptual convenience, but there is no single specific difference common to them all. Nevertheless, it is appropriate to group them in this way because they form a more or less continuous series in which any two neighbors may closely resemble each other yet not at all resemble the members at the other end of the series. (114-15)

This series itself is arbitrary, since any arrangement will depend on what traits are chosen as the basis of the arrangement; each individual romance intersects the other lines at different points, which thus allows for a broad range of elements within the larger genre. In keeping with this idea, I see no problem putting such outwardly dissimilar works as *Kyng Horn* and *Melusine* into the same genre, romance.

The Arthurian cycles incorporate a strong sense of history; their ultimate source, Geoffrey of Monmouth's *Historia*, was, to the dismay of a few insightful clerics, accepted by the general twelfth-century populace as true history. In addition, the cycles begin with the story of Joseph of Arimathea and the Christian elements of history. While both of these lines are today dismissed as fabrication, or legend, in their day their historicity was rarely questioned. This historical sense is usually associated with epic, as is the tragic end to the Arthurian saga, hence problem the first in using traditional classification: are the cycles epic or romance, or something undeserving of either name? Alongside this historical sense in the cycles, we find elements commonly attributed to romance. There is also the question of prose, generally associated with history and philosophy, here being used for a courtly narrative, instead of the traditional verse. The ambiguities add up under the common system of genre classification, leaving us in a no-man's land.

Coming on the heels of Chrétien and other romancers, the cycles clearly have no intrinsic tie to the traditional epic form; they may, however, owe something to the very much alive contemporary chansons de geste. The Vulgate Merlin in particular shares a concern for social order and anti-pagan warfare. But not the Huth. The milieu of each cycle is still a matter for debate, and knowing their origins would undoubtedly answer many questions. I am inclined to believe, however, that the writers of both cycles felt comfortable with their works. They had precedents all around them for whatever path they took--history, the marvellous, individual adventure, religious tasks, and so on. Each fit his work to his message--and here I must include Geoffrey and Malory as well--and did not allow a preconceived set of rules to dictate form. There has been a growing awareness in the second half of this century that we moderns must take medieval literature on its own terms and not project our standards, rules, or expectations back through the centuries.[3] This awareness has not, I believe, caught up entirely with medieval genre classifications, and the Hirschian continuum is my preference for an interim method.

In any case, for ease of reference, I would like to call the area on the continuum surrounding the cycles "legendary romance." A working description of this sub-genre includes: 1. The narrative builds from an historical context, Christian and/or pagan; the "history" can be more or less tied to actual ("true" in the modern sense) fact. 2. The original history/legend can be expanded or elaborated through peripheral or borrowed stories. 3. Romance elements (those described above in relation to Chrétien's texts) are adapted and incorporated as appropriate to the historical context and the author's contemporary situation and purpose.

The same awareness of a cultural gap applies as well to the medieval writer's use of various fantasy techniques, and understanding these tendencies will help in dealing with the problems of genre as well. In reading critics from the late nineteenth and early twentieth century, it is clear that one objection they have to the romance genre is its seemingly gratuitous use of fantasy. With a growing awareness in the society at large of the workings of fantasy (as in the psychological field), literary scholars have likewise become increasingly aware of its potential as a legitimate function of literature.

Like romance, fantasy resists narrow definition (Jackson 1), but here I must consider some trans-temporal ideas. One technique of fantasy literature applicable to romance is organizational symmetry. Several critics, beginning with Ferdinand Lot and Eugene Vinaver, have noted that medieval literature, while lacking the realistic logic we have come to expect in fiction, does function according to the logic of symmetry--repeated patterns, juxtaposition, and so on. Such organizational techniques are common to fantasy literature in all periods (Ryding 110). Once we recognize that the technique is shared by medieval romance, it should not be surprising (or gratuitous) that marvels are found there. Nor is it surprising that organizing fiction in such a way should have occurred; the techniques perform the same function then in romance as they do now in modern fantasy fiction.[4]

Other concerns and techniques shared by medieval romance and fantasy literature in general include the tendency of the protagonist to help others, a concern with moral and ethical conduct, a conscious or unconscious striving toward self-realization, a belief in magic, and a tendency to raise questions about the proper use of power (magical and otherwise). Fantasy also shows us "gaps" in our knowledge because of the special vantage-point its methods provide, gaps which stifle the path to self-realization. The techniques of fantasy can be used by different genres, so it is important to note the vast difference between the modern "fantasy genre" (itself usually classified within the romance mode) and the techniques which adapt to many times and forms. Frye comments as well that fantasy is "the normal technique for fiction writers who do not believe in the permanence or continuity of the society they belong to" (Secular Scripture 138). While the millennial apprehensions of the tenth century had faded by the thirteenth, it may be worthwhile pondering the attitudes of these authors toward their society if Frye's observation holds true.

One final note on fantasy and marvels; we must distinguish between what we perceive as fantasy and what the medieval audience would have perceived. True fantasy, as Schmerl observes (107), must be regarded as such by the author and his contemporaries. Thus, the mere existence of magic in a medieval text does not mean that that magic should be regarded as unreal. Certain abilities were granted practitioners then which are not granted today, and I attempt to shed some light on medieval perceptions, especially in the first chapter.

My first chapter, then, presents a general overview of medieval attitudes towards magic as revealed in historical texts, saints' lives, and some early vernacular texts. The second and third discuss Geoffrey of Monmouth's two works, the Historia Regum Britanniae and Vita Merlini, to look at the beginnings of the figure of Merlin and its two complementary strands. Chapter Four examines Merlin in the Vulgate cycle's second volume; Chapter Five, the Huth Suite du Merlin; Chapter Six, Malory.

Why focus on Merlin? Aside from the intrinsic fascination the figure has elicited over time, I found its presence within the Arthurian story seemed to affect--or perhaps reflect--the direction of a given work. Why is Merlin missing from Chrétien? A related question: Why are Chrétien's romances set in an ahistorical, distant "past," while the _Merlin_ texts are doubly tied to history? I believe the absence of the one influences the absence of the other. In addition, an observation by Robert Hanning concerning the changes he sees appearing in the thirteenth century is relevant. The narratives begin to represent, instead of individual fates, as in the twelfth century, a group fate--his specific reference is to the Arthurian saga and its apocalypse (_Individual_ 237). Hanning relates Merlin's re-entry to a move from one type of fantasy (mysterious) to another, the supernatural (miraculous), which is linked to the Grail plot line. In connection with this shift, he sees instead of a subjective, or person-centered, representation of time, an objective, or nation- (i.e. history-) centered time, which is indeed operating in the Arthurian cycles (200).

These two types of romances sit at different points on the continuum--Chrétien further from history or legend than the cycles--and the figure of Merlin, from the beginning, is tied to history and to the Christian religion in its most historical sense. While each work examined portrays a slightly different approach to the body of legend surrounding Merlin and his _confrères_, all of them share two things: first, a tension between the demonic and saintly elements in Merlin's portrayal; and second, a concern for ethics in the social structure, in the religious sphere, and, ultimately, in the individual.

Notes - Introduction

[1]Many terms have been used to describe the non-realistic elements in literature, some with very specific connotations. For the purposes of my work, I have adopted the following categories from Stevens' Medieval Romance:

1. General technique or presence - fantasy or marvels (with the accompanying terms fantastic, marvellous, merveilleux)
2. Man-manipulated - magical
3. God-manipulated - miraculous
4. No clear source - mysterious.

There will be occasional overlap, or doubt, as to categorization of specific incidents. As Poirion notes (96), there is often a hesitation between distinguishing "science" and "magic", the former having either positive or neutral implications, the latter usually negative (even diabolical) implications.

The theories of Frye, Toderov and Rabkin on The Fantastic are too narrowly developed to apply to medieval romance, or even the general Fantasy genre. I agree here with Jackson (25); Poirion (3); Zumthor, Essai (138); and Manlove (Schlobin, 28). (Philmus' article attacks Toderov's theory itself, offering several arguments concerning its lack of development.)

[2]This terminology indicates, perhaps unknowingly, agreement with Griffin's argument that "new" romance insists on historicity (59-62).

[3]See, for example, "The Poetry of Interlace," Chapter Five of Vinaver's Rise of Romance.

[4]For further elaboration, see Mobley, "Toward a Definition"; Scholes, Structural Fabulation; Thompson, "Modern Fantasy"; and Jameson, "Magical Narrative."

Chapter One

The Good Magician Before Merlin: Secular Tales and Saints' Lives

Before we examine the figure of Merlin proper, a brief study of similar figures in Celtic literature may help us later to understand some aspects of the primary figure and the types of romances in which he appears. In Merlin's portrayal at least two different, but not incompatible, literary traditions converge: (1) vernacular, secular Celtic tales, and (2) Celtic (i.e., early British and Irish) saints' lives. Both traditions display a variety of fantasy and contain magic-working figures. While wielders of magic are not unique to the Celtic world, the use here of only Celtic works will serve to emphasize the cultural and literary milieu into which Merlin is born.

A short advisory should be issued here, that my concern with the works in question is literary and, as much as possible, self-contained. No claim of influence, at least in specific terms of content and source-seeking, is made. As Pierre Le Gentil remarked in connection with the Didot Perceval, "Have not scholars, absorbed in the task of distinguishing the elements in the composition, failed to do justice to the composition itself?" (261) This background chapter means, then, to serve as an introduction to certain types of literary norms (such as have survived) in circulation at the time, because this kind of familiarity would have affected audience perceptions of Merlin. This approach will attempt to distinguish between the accretion of post-medieval views of Merlin and his talents, and the perception which might have been likely in the twelfth or thirteenth century.

Similarly, in the case of the secular stories especially, the question of mythological origins is not pertinent to the study here. Rachel Bromwich has noted that we know too little about Celtic myth to have a firm basis for interpretive studies, and "it is important to bear in mind that the debris of pagan Celtic religion had in large measure already lost its meaning for the redactors of Welsh and Irish tales even before they were transmitted to the Continent" ("Celtic Inheritance" 216-17). We have, I believe, a chance of recapturing the "meaning" of a Merlin figure by examining some parallels found in contemporary narrative texts and using these as a guide, rather than relying upon more modern information, guesses, and biases.

Some knowledge of the legal and religious views of the period toward magic and magicians can also shed light on the likely contemporary perceptions of such figures in literature. Both the Church and secular authorities in Britain and Ireland attempted to control the pagan practices of magic. At first, neither authority advocated the death penalty unless the crime of magic itself resulted in homicide, and the criminal refused to refrain from magic in the future.[1] One entry in the law codes of Aethalstan II (reigned ca. 925-939 [?]) reads:

> 6. And we have declared with regard to witchcrafts and sorceries and deadly spells, if death is occasioned

> thereby, and [the accused] cannot deny it [the charge], that he shall forfeit his life. #1. If, however, he wishes to deny it, and is found guilty in the threefold ordeal, he shall remain in prison for 120 days; and afterwards the relatives may take him out and give 120 shillings to the king and pay the wergeld [of the dead man] to his relatives, and stand as surety for the offender that he shall cease from such practices for ever. (Attenborough 131)[2]

Irish laws and church penitential manuals also bear witness to a continued struggle against magical practices, and such crimes are often not a class in themselves but are dealt with in conjunction with other crimes such as "brigandage, druidism, and satirizing; further, adultery, incest, perjury, heresy. . ." (Bieler 278). Recommended punishment for these crimes varies from a month to seven years on bread and water (Bieler 101, 104, 160).

Unlike the early English and Irish law codes, the Welsh codes contain no references to witches, seers, or magicians. However, these early Welsh codes maintain a clear distinction between delict, the King's jurisdiction, and sin, which is the Church's.[3] The Church probably was the arena for magical "crimes," hence the lack of provision in the secular laws. In any case, where the early medieval laws in Britain and Ireland do concern themselves with magic, it is usually where the practice results in harm to some person or his property. Although the Church in theory assumed all magic drew upon demons for help,[4] "benevolent magic," according to Jeffrey Russell, "was often tacitly allowed to exist" (Witchcraft 13). As will be seen below in the discussion of saints' lives, Christianity itself contained some "magical" elements in its outward forms.

By advertising its concern, the Church itself gave magic a heightened--perhaps artificial--importance, and interest in the processes of magic increased during the twelfth century (Wagner 98). From the end of the eleventh century on, magic gradually filtered its way into literature, first with divination, leading to "enchantemens" and finally to a whole new type of creature best exemplified by the faery king Oberon in _Huon of Bourdeaux_ (Wagner 62). During this period, the Church became more and more overt in its struggle against magic, divination, and finally witchcraft. The Church in the mid-eleventh century might simply have blamed events--with occasional informal condemnation--on sorcery. By the early years of the thirteenth century, provincial councils officially condemned "les _magi_, les _divinatores_, et les _invocatores daemonum_," closely identifying magic with heresy (Wagner 50).[5] In practice, however, the layman, apart from the synods and councils of the Church's high officials, distinguished between acceptable _beneficium_ and unacceptable _maleficium_. Tolerance was more common than not--again with the exception of harmful results. Magic was a living idea (Peters 46, 116-17),[6] and its inclusion in the aristocratic literature of the period was not unusual; rather, I would argue that particularly in the case of Merlin such inclusion is a reflection of some dominant interests of the time.

The Four Branches of the Mabinogi are, it is generally agreed, the earliest surviving Welsh prose narratives, linguistically dated ca. 1100, though preserved only in fourteenth-century manuscripts (Williams viii-xx). These four stories[7] contain a representative sample of the kinds of magic and fantasy found in secular Celtic tales. The most common type of magic in these stories, absent alone in Branwen, is shape-changing, followed by magical or mysterious items and personal attributes. There is one case of prophecy and some use of the curse as a manifestation of power, which are more prominent in saints' lives, discussed below.

Math contains the greatest number of shape-changing incidents. To deceive Pryderi, the disguised Gwydion conjures up horses and dogs, then golden shields out of mushrooms;[8] in a later episode he creates ships and shoe-leather out of sea plants (PKM 79). With Math's assistance, Gwydion forms Lleu's wife Blodeuedd:

> Ac yna y kymeryssant wy blodeu y deri, a blodeu y banadyl, a blodeu yr erwein, ac o'r rei hynny, asswynaw yr un uorwyn deccaf a thelediwaf a welas dyn eiroet. (PKM 83)
>
> (So they took the flowers of oak, broom, and meadow sweet, and from these they created the fairest and most beautiful maiden anyone ever saw.[9])

In order to circumvent two of Aranrhod's three curses on her son Lleu, Gwydion transforms his own and Lleu's appearances (PKM 79, 81). Math, however, shows the strongest changing-power, to which Gwydion himself must submit. In punishing Gwydion and his brother Gilfaethwy for the violation of Goewin and the war against Dyfed, Math transforms the brothers into pairs of animals (deer, boar, and wolves) for a year in each form. The transformation is total, for the two have offspring in each form, and Math changes the three young animals into human form when they are brought to him (PKM 74-76). Later in the story, Lleu flies off changed into an eagle (involuntarily, it seems), wounded after an attempt on his life. Gwydion must find the bird/Lleu and return him to human form (PKM 89-90). Gwydion then punishes Blodeuedd for her role in that murder attempt by changing her permanently into an owl (PKM 91).

The other shape-changing incidents occur in _Pwyll_, when Arawn and Pwyll exchange roles for a year, and in _Manawydan_, when Llwyd's court, in the form of mice, ravage Manawydan's grain fields. Also, Llwyd himself appears in three guises attempting to rescue his wife. Both of these masters of magic, Arawn and Llwyd, have overtones of Otherworld domicile, but neither Math (who is seen as king of the historical kingdom of Gwynedd) nor his nephew Gwydion are Otherworldly.[10] In fact, Math and Gwydion resemble Pwyll (King of Dyfed) and Manawydan more closely than they do the other magicians in their roles. Gwydion and Manawydan specifically share a place among the Three Golden Shoemakers[11] (PKM 54, 81), for example, and each is accomplished in other crafts and on the battlefield as well.

Generally, the magic found in the _Mabinogi_ (speaking of magic, again, as manipulated by a person, not that found in inanimate objects or working without specific direction) is of a neutral nature, even tending toward the beneficent. It basically follows the tradition of _beneficium_ or white magic, which "pursues the ethics of kindness and goodness; it represents the self-effacement of the will of the individual [magician] toward the acquisition of glory or power." In contrast, _maleficium_ "in its mildest application seeks the selfish advancement of an individual; in its most hateful aspect, it is vindictive and destructive" (C. Loomis 4). This malevolent magic also occurs in the Mabinogi, but is overcome in the end. Perhaps the most striking examples are the desolation of Dyfed and the later capture of Pryderi and Rhiannon through Llwyd's spells (his revenge for a friend's insult years before) in Manawydan.

> A guedy y bwyta kyntaf y nos honno, tra uei y gwassanaethwyr yn bwyta, kyuodi allan a orugant, a chyrchu Gorssed Arberth[12] a wnaethant yll pedwar, ac yniuer gyt ac wynt. Ac ual y bydant yn eisted yuelly, llyma dwrwf, a chan ueint y twrwf, llyma gawat o nywl yn dyuot hyt na chanhoed yr un ohonunt wy y gilid. Ac yn ol y nwyl, llyma yn goleuhau pob lle. A phan edrychyssant y ford y guelyn y preideu, a'r anreitheu, a'r kyuanhed kyn no hynny, ny welynt neb ryw dim, na thy, nac aniueil, na mwc, na than, na dyn, na chyuanhed, eithyr tei y llys yn wac, diffeith, anghyuanhed, heb dyn, heb uil yndunt. . . . (PKM 51-52)

> (And after the first feeding that night, while the attendants were eating, they strolled out, the four of them, and went to the mound of Arberth, and the host with them. As they were sitting, there was a tumultuous clatter, and concurrent with the sound, a mist falling, so that not one of them could see the other. After the mist, then, it brightened everywhere. And when they looked in the places where they had seen flocks and cattle and habitations before then, no one could see anything whatsoever--neither house, nor animal, nor smoke, nor fire, nor dwellings, only the court buildings, and those empty, deserted, desolate, without men or animals in them. [Ford 77])

Gwydion does use magic against Pryderi, first to deceive and soon after to kill him in battle, but Math punishes him for it, and the primary use of Gwydion's magic involves helping Lleu against the animosity of Aranrhod and Blodeuedd.

At the end of Branwen, we hear that by use of a magic mantle Caswallawn has killed six of the leaders of Britain and thereafter is crowned king himself (PKM 46). Primarily, however, magic in these stories justly punishes or outwits an opponent. In either case, magic is only another weapon, to be used or misused according to the character of the wielder.

Significantly, the magician is not the primary character in any of these tales, but plays a secondary, supporting role. Gwydion, whose prominence is greater than the other magicians', himself gives way before Lleu, to whose birth and youth the story progresses and whose future as ruler of Gwynedd is the concern of the story's final lines. This supporting role of magic and magicians is demonstrated by the fact that the major emphasis of each story lies elsewhere, centering around a character who is not a magician.

Again, the most obvious example is found in Manawydan. Here, the primary character, Manawydan, not only is not a magician himself, but he outwits a character who is. Manawydan succeeds throughout in maintaining his equanimity in spite of the desolation of his new home, the enmity of rival craftsmen, and eventually the loss of his wife and step-son by magic--all of this on top of the tragic events of Branwen, through which he lost family and nation.

Manawydan's other virtues, too, center around his ability to control himself. He uses common sense when confronting the unknown; he does not rashly follow Pryderi inside the mysterious fort, whereas Rhiannon does and is captured herself (PKM 56-57). Gruffydd, in his study Rhiannon, has compared Manawydan's character and story with those of St. Eustace, whose Life was disseminated widely in the middle ages (73). Both lose property and family, travel after the loss, and are re-united with the family after due suffering and patient restraint in the face of adversity. In keeping with the moral concern of the saint's life, and equally of the secular tale, in neither case is the primary concern the fantastic circumstances of loss and recovery, but rather the way in which the characters stand up under adverse conditions. In Manawydan's case, the same strength of character and wisdom which carried him, and the others, through exile and hard times, also helps him succeed in outwitting Llwyd and finally recovering all that was lost.

Each story of the *Mabinogi* is in one sense a variation on the theme of friendship; as each story progresses we see how, in this world, ill actions beget ill results, and good actions good results (Gantz 249, 254). In *Math*, the plot to bring about the rape of Goewin leads to the war with Dyfed, and the adultery of Blodeuedd and Gronw leads to the murder attempt on Lleu. Both Pwyll, with Arawn's wife, and Manawydan, left alone in Dyfed with Pryderi's wife Cigfa, are chaste, and this control, seen in the light of friendship and its concurrent honesty, bodes well for both Pwyll and Manawydan. *Math* and *Branwen* both offer contrasts to the other two stories; where in *Pwyll* and *Manawydan* the mood is one of positive accomplishment, the mood in *Branwen* is tragic and in *Math* it is ambivalent at best.

Although Math ends on the positive note of Lleu's future, the shadow of broken ties is cast over the whole (not least of which is Lleu's mother's animosity towards him), in contrast to Pwyll and Manawydan which both end in the formation and reaffirmation of close ties of loyalty, family and friendship. The magic and other fantastic elements are but narrative devices which contribute to the progression of the story lines. They never usurp center stage from the moral didacticism, which, to some extent, they disguise and make entertaining. Such a sweetening of the moral pill helps to make a lasting impression on the audience by shifting the scene outside the realm of daily life, hence into the exotic and memorable, a tactic not ignored by the writers of saints' lives.

The authors of saints' lives, too, used fantasy as a literary device to catch and sustain interest. The Bollandist Hippolyte Delehaye described the typical hagiographer as follows:

> Inspiration apart, hagiographers do just as poets do: they affect complete independence of, sometimes a lordly contempt for, historical facts; for real persons they substitute strongly-marked types; they borrow from anywhere in order to give color to their narrative and to sustain interest; above all, they are ever mindful of the marvellous, so apt for heightening the effect of an edifying subject (144).

The Celtic saints' lives which are closely contemporary to the Mabinogi (as well as to Geoffrey of Monmouth) contain many familiar Celtic fantastic elements. Although some of the elements discussed are not unique to Celtic saints' lives, it is crucial to note these elements were not foreign to the Celtic Christian culture and peoples, or their literary products, but similar to--or occasionally the same as--the stories circulating in the secular, indigenous culture.[14]

Several elements of the native culture were easily adapted to Christianity when in the second to fifth centuries missionary priests began the conversion in the Celtic areas of Britain. Leslie Hardinge, commenting on the way in which saints seemed to be successors of the Druids, drew up the following list of external (i.e., highly visible) similarities between the two.

> Both had seasons in which fires were ceremonially extinguished, and were then relighted from a symbolic flame. Both baptised infants, at which time the child's name was bestowed upon it. Both claimed to work magical cures, to predict events, and to transfer diseases from human beings to plants or other objects. Both were teachers of youth and counsellors of kings. Like the druid, the Christian soul-friend might banish a sinner (139).

Given Christianity's renowned abilities to assimilate native culture, once the priest overcame initial opposition, he could find it easy to supplant the pagan beliefs by using native custom to bind his position in the community. This is not to say he would go unopposed. St. Carannog, says his _Life_, was given the honors of a druid counsellor among the kings in Ireland, but "inuitis cetibus magorum."[15] The struggle against pagan beliefs, however, was most successful where it involved a transferral rather than a destruction of such ideas, and many of the saints' miracles are difficult to distinguish from feats of secular magic.[16]

A particularly telling example comes from the late seventh-century _Vita Columbani_ of Adomnan, which shows the saint contending with the magic of a group of druids in Scotland. These druids have vowed to detain Columba's ship by calling up a storm with their magical powers.

> Sanctus die eadem sicut corde proposuit ad lacum Nisae fluminis longum multa prosequente caterva venit. Magi vero gaudere tum coepere, magnam videntes superinductam caliginem et contrarium cum tempestate flatum.
> Nec mirum haec interdum arte daemonum posse fieri, deo permittente, ut etiam venti et equora in asperius concitentur. . . .
> Noster itaque Columba videns contra se elimenta concitari furentia Christum invocat dominum. . . . Et post haut grande intervallum venti contrarii ad iteneris ministeria cum omnium ammiratione revertuntur. (405, 407)

The druids are clearly "granted" the power to set against the saint that he might overcome it, but what might be confusing is the precise difference between reciting a spell (i.e., calling on demonic help) and Columba's "call on Christ the Lord." To someone not attuned to theological niceties, the distinction is merely between two different kinds of magical power, one stronger than the other.[17] Though the saints and their followers believe and proclaim that their power comes to them from a "higher source," outwardly it looks the same as the personal magic of the pagan.

The shape-shifting seen in the _Mabinogi_ and which is also found in the Merlin texts is common in both Irish and Welsh secular texts. Cú Chulainn, in the story of the _Táin Bó Cúailnge_, encounters King Buan's daughter the Morrígan in four different forms (an eel, she-wolf, heifer and old woman) (194-97).[18] In the same cycle, a pair of swineherds adept in "pagan arts" fight over a period of years in a succession of eight forms, ranging from maggots to birds to phantoms.[19] This same type of successive-form battle occurs in the

Welsh tale of Gwion Bach[20] in which Gwion Bach flees from the wrath of the witch Ceridwen in various forms, and she chases in appropriate superior forms, until finally as a hen she swallows him in the form of a grain of wheat; he eventually is reborn as the poet-prophet Taliesin (Ford 162-63). In Cwlhwch and Olwen (ca. 1050), we are told that one of Arthur's men, Gwrhyr, goes in the shape of a bird to the boar Twrch Trwyth (himself a former king reduced to this form "for his sins" [Ford 153]).

Surprisingly enough, one finds examples of shape-changing in a few saints' lives, too. Usually such transformation in a saint's life would be of a disguised devil, or as a result of a demon's work. For a saint to cause a change himself is not common, but the Vita Sancti Coemgeni (14th-century manuscript, but Life dates from the 7th) offers two such examples. One time Coemgen sees twelve men coming to find and kill him, and he runs to elude them.

> Videns ipse eos se sequentes, prostrauit se ad terram iuxta ostium. . . . Venientes autem inimici, nichil ibi de homine sentierunt, set tantum lignum transuersum super terram.[21]

Perhaps in this passage the saint (or rather God) merely caused the would-be assassins to see only a log, without an actual transformation. But a second incident, in which Coemgen protects friends whose enemies have followed them to the saint, leads me to interpret these actions as true shape-changing:

> Et veniens inter insidias inimicorum suorum, apparuit ipse cum suis in formis et in uelocitate ceruorum; et sic euasit ille ab ini[mi]cis suis incolumis per benedictionem viri Dei. (VSH 252)

The echoes of secular shape-shifting, like that which we see in the _Mabinogi_, are strong, especially when compounded with the numerous other examples of shared magical or mysterious events. St. Abban, in one case, changed the sex of a baby from female to male out of pity for an old man with no other heirs (VSH 19), and Brendan saved a man by making him look like a stone--while the pursuers cut off the "head" of a stone which appeared to be the man (VSH 101).

The secular stories reveal a great belief in the efficacy of blessings and curses; in the _Mabinogi_ we find Aranrhod's three curses on her son, the last of which, especially, must be met by the use of magic if Lleu is to have a wife. Irish tales, too, abound with curses, and it is difficult to distinguish among the styles of Irish cursing, Gwydion's conjuring and Aranrhod's cursing. The contest between Cú Chulainn and the Morrígan, mentioned above, began as a bout of curse-vows. Sometimes cursing took the form of "satire" (_aer_), where the purpose was to shame the subject; with such purpose Medb sent messengers to insult the warrior Fer Diad (_Táin_ 211-12). Such maledictions were taken seriously (Fer Diad agrees to fight his foster-brother rather than be satirized), and the laws in Ireland put careful limits on the legal use of satires (Robinson 103). In particular, the laws did not maintain a distinction between magical maledictions and mockery-satires; either one was easy to abuse and such abuses were a "common form of injury" in Irish legal proceedings and carried the punishment of a misdemeanor (Robinson 105). Both the Irish and Welsh styles of satire or cursing, in effect, are active uses of magic and this impression is little changed in the saints' lives.

Saints traditionally call upon the power of God to bless people, reward them for some action, heal the sick and so on, and we read many passages where Celtic saints practice this kind of beneficent use of power. Saints, however, do not always bless, and Charles Plummer, in his introduction to a collection of saints' lives from Ireland, remarks on the unusual "maledictions and vindictiveness of Celtic saints" (cxxv).[22] Several saints call upon God to destroy people unkind to them, much as Old Testament prophets called down destruction upon the enemies of Israel. While still young, the Welsh saint Cadog calls down the wrath of God on a boorish man who made him carry hot coals in his cloak (VSB 36-38). In another use of the curse, Mochuda berates a man who mocked him, and reverses the common "fertility blessing:"

> [Dulach] winked mockingly with one of his eyes; moreover, he laughed and behaved irreverently towards Mochuda. Mochuda said to him: "Thus shall you be--with one eye closed and a grin on your countenance--to the end of your life; and of your descendants many will be similarly afflicted."[23]

Cadog even curses two of his own disciples who have left behind one of his books. In anger, he sends them back to retrieve it, adding, "Ite, nunquam redituri." On their return trip with the book, the disciples' boat overturns, drowning them, but the saint still recovers his book, undamaged, from inside a fish (VSB 92).

The curse as a tool of power can simply chasten, too. The following passage from the <u>Vita Sancti Kebii</u> is but one example of many in which temporary blindness is used to show the strength and superiority of the saints' Lord and of the saints' faith and calling.

> Et confestim surrexit Ethelic cum omni familia sua eicere monachos de terra sua. Et protinus cedidit Ethelic de equo suo in uia, et statim mortuus est equus eius. Et cecus fuit Ethelic statim, et tota familia eius. Tunc Ethelic prostrauit se in faciem suam, deditque corpus et animam suam Deo et sancto Kepio. Et statim per orationem sancti Kepii sanati sunt uiri Ethelic et ipse et equus eius. (VSB 236)

In the _Vita Sancti Paterni_ a local _tirannus_ by the name of Arthur covets one of the saint's tunics and tries with a group of his men to take it. Padarn, hearing of this, suggests, "Immo absorbeat eum tellus," and Arthur is immediately up to his chin in the earth. Arthur repents and begs forgiveness, whereupon he is set free (VSB 260). Such lessons in manners and in faith are plentiful in the lives, but they are balanced, first, by the forgiveness of the saints, and second, by the many acts of blessing and aid to the same saints' credit.

Undoubtedly, the marvellous in both directions is used to impress, to show both the power of God and the faithful behavior that power demands. Miracles are essential to a saint's life, for they give necessary evidence that the supernatural is at work, and the most forceful impression on people's minds comes through the eyes, from actually seeing the "effects of Grace" (Delehaye, 33). The didactic nature of these works is very clear in such passages. The saints' lives were not solely, or even primarily, biographies as the modern world conceives of that genre; the lives are too full of traditional, generic conventions to be coincident with history on all points. Like a secular legend, the lives substitute an idealized portrait for a realistic one, including an "eschewing of historical truth with regard to geography and chronological sequence, a hyperbolic stress on the marvellous, . . . and an idealization of the hero into a personified abstraction or type" (Lagorio, "Pan-Brittonic" 31).

The biographical pose coupled with the religious didactic purposes leaves ample room for the effective use of the marvellous to increase both a character's standing and the impact of the narrative. Although fantasy plays a small part in the narrative progression in a saint's life (which tends to be episodic anyway) in comparison with the secular stories, it is prominent because it surrounds the major character, the saint.

Unlike the secular magician, the saint-magician is always the protagonist of the narrative in which he appears. D. T. Childress notes in her article, "Between Romance and Legend," that "saints and romance heroes . . . have different kinds of control over their environment". One important distinction she notes is that "preternatural marvels are more often in the world around the romance hero" rather than originating in him or his personal abilities (313). The saint combines the active power of the magician with the passive role of the hero. Whereas both hero and saint encounter situations in which they must overcome opposition, the ways each accomplishes this differ. The saint can resort to direct divine intervention, but the romance hero must depend on his human skills--compare Cadog's recovery of his book from the fish and Manawydan's recovery of Pryderi from Llwyd.

Another characteristic shared by the Celtic saint's life and secular tale is the narrative's predilection for following the protagonist from birth (or even before it). Pryderi and Lleu are chronicled thus in the Mabinogi, and a number of Irish heroes, Cú Chulainn among them, are as well. It is not unusual for the conception and birth of a hero to be on the fringes of or outside socially acceptable behavior, supernatural or not. Aranrhod was being tested as a virgin when she suddenly dropped her sons Lleu and Dylan (PKM 77); Pryderi's parents were acceptably married, but the supernatural kidnapping on the night of his birth led to Rhiannon being accused of infanticide (PKM 20-21).

In the case of St. David of Wales, Rhygyvarch tells how the saint's father, a king, came together with the mother.

> [V]irtus diuina misit Sanctum, regem Ceretice regionis, usque ad plebem Demetice gentis. Inuentique rex obuiam sibi sanctimonialem, nomine Nonnitam uirginem, puellam pulcram nimis et decoram, quam concupiscens tetigit ui oppressam, et concepit filium suum Dauit agium, que nec antea nec postea uirum agnouit, sed in castitate mentis et corporis perseuerans fidelissimam duxit uitam. (6)

Although the rape resulted in a saint, the conception and bastard birth were hardly in the realm of the "socially acceptable" (though no doubt it very much reflected social reality). Cadog, too, was the result of an abduction, although his parents were married before his birth (VSB 26-28).

A singular case of similarity between secular tale and saints' lives can be seen in various versions of a birth delayed in response to a prediction and the consequent effect on the child. When St. Molasius' mother was in labor, a magician advised her that if the birth could be delayed by one day, the child would be

> illustrious and for a great dignity, and miraculous, righteous, very noble and be an offspring profitable for the salvation of the world's most western portion. . . . The Very God retained the birth in Monoa's womb, so that, just when the sun was risen on the morrow, she brought forth. . . upon a certain flagstone. ("Life of St. Molasius" 19)

A pagan element can immediately be seen in the person of the magician (not a Christian holy man) who pronounced the prophecy. But comparing the tale with a passage in the Irish story of "The Battle of Magh mucramha" reveals more parallels. In this story, the daughter of the magician Dil gives birth to Fiacha Muillethan, and his name is explained in the following passage.

> As regards the epithet muillethan, or "broad crown", the occasion of his being so styled was this: at ath Nemthenn on the Suir [as she drove the wizard's chariot], the pains of labor assailed Dil's daughter Moncha, and her father said: "an ill thing it is that thou art not brought to bed to-morrow morning instead of today for, had it been then, that which is now to be born should for ever have overtopped all Ireland." "True it is," she answered: "therefore unless that the offspring break out through one or other of my sides, by no other way shall it win forth at all!" Into the water she went down from them, and bestrid a stone that is in the mid ford: "maintain thou me," she cried to the rock, and to the hour of tierce upon the morrow there she held fast. "It is time," her father said; they loosed her hold for her, and her lips faded [i.e., she died]; but the babe's head had been flattened against the stone. (354-55)

In Molasius' birth, the mother had no stone to help her, nor was the child's head deformed. The birth was, however, upon a "flagstone," and was delayed in concert with a favorable prophecy. The closest resemblance of a saint's birth to the secular one I have found occurs in the Life of St. Aed.

> Cumque illa esset vicina partui super sanctum Edum, quidam propheta venit secus domum illius, et dixit ille suis: "Est mulier istius domus pregnans, cuius tempus ut pariat uenit. Si igitur infans, quem in vtero habet, cras nasceretur hora matutina, magnus esset coram Deo et hominibus, in celo et in terra. . . ." Hoc audiens quedam puella, ilico uenit, et retulit domine sue, incipienti tunc parturire. Illa ait: "Vere, nisi per latera mea venerit, non egredietur ex utero meo, donec illa hora veniet." Et sedit super petram, mansitque in ea sedens usque ad horam matutinam contra dolores parturicionum. Hoc magnum mirabile fecit Deus in natiuitate sancti Edi infantis. Nam cum mater eius hora matutina fatigata esset, capud infantis super petram cecidit, et fecit concauum in ea secundum similitudinem capitis. (VSH 34)

The only substantial change in the story is the effect of the child's head upon the stone. The miracle of the mother's staying-power here is compounded by the infant saint's first miracle. The same infant's miracle is found at St. Declan's birth (Power 9), and in both cases water which collected in the resulting hollow was said to be effective in cures.

Where Celtic saints' lives include stories regarding the youth of saints, the emphasis is necessarily on different attributes than we find in secular tales. Where, for example, Cú Chulainn's training and increasing prowess at arms is detailed, Saint Cadog's progress in Latin and attendance at church are among the religious author's topics (VSB 32-36). Saint David's education, too, consists of "psalmos, lectiones totius anni, et missas et sinaxin," and he goes on to further instruction and becomes a scribe (Rhygyvarch, 8-9). Illtud begins his life less assiduously devoted to religion, for after an early education "in septem disciplinis" he turns to a military and married life, renowned for his skill and intelligence, before adopting the monastic life (VSB 194-96, 200).

Although a monk/saint cannot be a ruling monarch or lord under the conditions these saints' lives propound,[24] his standing in a community can be elevated to similar status in several ways. Some saints may be sons, or more distant relatives, of rulers. Saints Cadog, Carannog, Tatheus and Gwynllyw are all sons of kings (as is David, albeit bastard), and Illtud is the grandson of a king. Some later versions of St. David's life trace his lineage back to the Biblical Family of David, i.e., the line of the Holy Family (Buched Dewi 1). St. Gwynllyw began as a king, indeed was Cadog's father, but when he turned to the religious life he gave up his kingdom (VSB 176).[25]

Other saints show in their contact with kings that they are superior to them, at least in matters spiritual or pertaining to the religious community, and often in more mundane matters as well. Where the major characters of the Mabinogi and Irish tales possess the superior status of birth and talent (often reinforced in the course of the narrative, as with Gwydion and Manawydan), so too the saints prove their worth, through induced and spontaneous acts of God on their behalf.

When one ruler appropriates St. Brynach's prize cow, he finds the meat cannot be cooked because the water over a fire remains cold (VSB 12). Only with St. Cadog's help does one prince escape some enemies when trapped (VSB 80). The passage quoted above from the

Vita Sancti Kebii shows the king and household struck blind and helpless when they attempt to attack the saint. Several saints successfully avert prolonged wars; Padarn, for example, is brought in to end the fighting between two kings in Ireland:

> At tunc temporis in Hibernia reges duarum prouinciarum discordant. . . . Tandem misericors Arbiter orbis, solita misertus prouidentia causam insperate pacis ad episcopum . . . mittit. Et ait, "Nisi uterque exercitus uultus sancti nuper ex Bruttannia uenientis uiderit, nunquam placabuntur ad inuicem reges maliciosi." Extimplo legati mittuntur. Paternum honorifice aduocant. Exercitus conuocantur. Paternum in medio statuunt. Gratia uultus eius diaboli discordie propelluntur. Pax perpetua inter utrasque prouincias oritur. . . . (VSB 254-56)

Among the Welsh saints, King Maelgwn seems to be their most common opponent; no less than three saints are forced to teach him lessons. Cadog convinces him to abandon an unjust war (VSB 74); Padarn reveals the king in a false accusation in trial by boiling water (VSB 258); and Cybi wins the life of a wild goat being hunted by the king (VSB 246).

When St. David settles into the area of Hoddnant (Rosina Vallis), he encounters a campaign of opposition from a "satrapus magusque," Baia, and his wife. The couple ends up dead after a series of unsuccessful attempts on the religious community's safety and repeated ridicule of their Christian morality (Rhygyvarch 10-13). In the process, Baia's stock are decimated, but after allowing David tenure on the land, Baia finds his animals restored to life. Later the wife murders her step-daughter and flees. Baia's resentment against David leads him to try to kill the saint, but he himself is killed on the way by an enemy. Essentially, Baia loses family, goods and life in his continued opposition to the saint, and unlike the honest Manawydan, does not regain them. We will see a similar loss in the story of Merlin's grandparents in Robert de Boron's work.

Where Padarn is able by the Grace of God to stop a war by his mere presence, Cadog's peace-making between King Arthur and a local chief, Legessauc (who had raided Arthur's cattle and caused the death of some men), takes a more active type of arbitration. A group of judges suggests that the recompense for Arthur's dead should be 100 cows. Arthur obstreperously requires particular coloration for these cows, and Cadog

> imperauit iuuenibus de concilio quatinus ix., siue, uelut quidam fatentur, c. iuuencas, ad se minare, cuiuscunque coloris forent. . . . [D]iuino magnalio ex praua Arthurii cupidine, in prelibatis coloribus pro beniuolo iustorum precatu ac desiderio statim mutata fuere. . . . Compulit igitur illas eotenus occurreruntque eis Arthurius, Chei at Bedguur, ceteris in littore sedentibus. At Chei et Bedguur gliscentes eas manibus ad litus alterum per cornua trahere, sed extimplo inter ipsorum manus, cunctis uidentibus, diuino nutu in filicis fascibus transfigurate sunt. Quod prodigium Arthurius aspectans, ut sibi dimitt(er)etur iniuria, quam illi irrogauerat, beatum uirum humiliter flagitauit. (VSB 70)

This active intervention in affairs can also be seen in a short passage in Carannog's Vita, in which the saint, in exchange for some information, subdues a serpent which had eluded King Arthur (VSB 144).

In all these proofs of a saint's power, there is no impression that they are undergoing the testings of character so common to secular stories. Initiations, and concurrently the type of humiliating tests secular heroes often encounter seem rare in Celtic saints' lives. In Pwyll's encounter with Arawn, Pryderi's entrapment in the enchanted mound, Lleu's wounding by Gronw, and other episodes in the *Mabinogi*, humiliation is a key element in each hero's learning process. A saint, however, is very rarely humiliated, and then never in his role as God's representative. The agent, too, of any reproof is usually not a lay person, but an angelic voice, dream, or a fellow religious; it is not unknown, either, to have one saint (generally the one whose life is being told) prove wiser or "stronger" than another saint. One example can be seen in the *Vita Sancti Cadoci*, when Gildas refuses to sell Cadog a certain bell and finds it subsequently will not ring again until Cadog finally does receive it (VSB 84-86). But Cadog, too, when angered at David's calling of a synod in his absence, is admonished by an angel, who reminds Cadog that, "Qui odit fratrem suum homicida est," upon which reminder Cadog promptly forgives David the insult (VSB 60).

In this aspect of proof and testing, the saint particularly shares more the role of the magician, who also is rarely humiliated, than the role of the hero, whose development depends upon risking the perils of defeat in order to overcome them and emerge a stronger character. This difference is (perhaps unduly) presented clearly to a modern reader in the several saints' lives where King Arthur appears; the king is always bested by the saint. Cadog outwits him over the cattle; Padarn causes him to be swallowed in earth to his chin; Carannog subdues the serpent Arthur was unable to overcome.

In the Mabinogi, where the magicians are beaten, the circumstances are similar to those when a saint is reprimanded. Both Llwyd and Gwydion misuse their talents and are justly punished by a "higher authority"--in Gwydion's case by his uncle the king, in Llwyd's by the righteous Manawydan. We will see this characterization of the magician adapted to the figure of Merlin.

I wish to note a few independent episodes in these Celtic saints' lives for the sake of recognition later in this study. The first concerns saints who speak "prematurely": St. Barrus speaks from the womb (VSH 66), and several others speak as infants, including Ninian, Albeus and German (C. Loomis 24, 142), as Merlin will. Second, before Cadog persuades Maelgwn to break off the war, he brings a dark mist into the king's camp, so thick that one man could not see another (VSB 74); Merlin performs a similar feat several times as he helps Arthur's army. Finally, although I have not detailed the gifts of foreknowledge and prophecy, these saints' lives (like those of other times and places) are full of examples of saints both knowing events beforehand and knowing about events at a distance at the same time they happen, and this type of knowledge is a basic component of Merlin's powers.

The fact that these types of events and those detailed above are seen in saints' lives at approximately the same time as the role of Merlin is developing sheds light on an aspect of his character which could be missed otherwise. The way in which Christianity took over as the dominant religion was not purely theological, in Britain or elsewhere. One must remember, too, that the medieval church was not that of Vatican II or even that of the Counter-Reformation. Just as the missionary priests in Ireland found Christianity adapted easily into the former Druidic and other cultural niches, so too did it adapt at other points in time. Jeffrey Russell, in his history of the growth of the ideas of witchcraft and magic, notes that

> new religions often consider the practices of older religions as magic: the Christian attitude that paganism, whether Greco-Roman, Germanic, or Celtic, was magical and diabolical, failed to recognize the distinction between magic and religion among those people themselves. . . . Christianity itself was scarcely free from magical conceptions, high or low. Prayers were used as incantations, God and the saints were compelled by threats, the sacraments were used for magical purposes, and wonders were sought often without distinguishing between magic and miracle. (Witchcraft 11)

The distinctive change which the dominance of Christianity, through the literary medium of the saint's life, seems to have wrought in the romance-epics is primarily a transferral of the motivation of the story from the earthly realms to the divine.[26] We see, too, that as the romance genre ages, the types of magic, fantasy, and mystery change, and at the same time gain in frequency. The earthly "fée" creatures move from the short Breton lais into the longer romances of chivalry, and are found alongside holy hermits and Christian miracles. Where once may have been seers and "scientists" (men learned in nature and its laws) soon are found the faery kingdom of Oberon (Wagner 98-99). It seems clear, from both the literary and ecclesiastical evidence, that interest in magic was very much alive in the eleventh to thirteenth centuries; indeed, just after the two French Merlin texts are estimated to have been written, the Councils of Tours and Trèves (1238) renewed the church's condemnation of magical practices (Wagner 100).[27]

Although the Church and its communicants may not have acknowledged the existence of magical elements in the Church itself, the adaptations seen in the Celtic lives of saints make it clear that the same kinds of acts, acceptable when performed by a religious, indicated pagan magic in the hands of a layman or a non-believer. It is implied, as well, that any convert must foreswear such acts if he has practiced them in the past.[28] The future portrayal of Merlin can be confusing on this basis: are his magical actions acceptable or not? Why or why not? The answers grow clearer as the legend builds, but his initial literary appearance in Geoffrey of Monmouth's Historia Regum Britanniae presents the problematic nature of this figure and provides few direct answers.

Notes - Chapter One

[1]Changes begin to appear, intermittently, with Alfred's reign in the late ninth century. See Russell, Witchcraft 73.

[2]See also p. 27 (Laws of Wihtred of Kent, ca. 695) and p. 109 (Edward and Guthrum, ca. 921-25).

[3]See Ellis 195-196; and Owen, Ancient Laws and Institutes of Wales.

[4]From at least the time of St. Augustine, the Church strove to distinguish between the miracles of demons and the miracles of God. Augustine spelled out his ideas in Books 8 to 10 of De civitate Dei, stating specifically that all magic, black or white, has one engaged in the rites of demons (Book 10, Chap. 9). He also condemns the belief that miracles are involved in using herbs or stones to promote healing and that divining by use of sacrificial animals or the sky is true (Book 10, Chap. 11). Later, Isidore of Seville in his Etymologiae also states that marvels can be effected through magic and the help of demons, and condemns it strongly (Book 8, Chap. 9). However, he saw no harm in stones with marvellous powers such as healing (Book 6). See also Thorndike, Chapter I.

[5]On the development of terminology: Latin--incantatores, daemonum invocatores, and magi are all relatively interchangeable; French--magie and nigromancie for the practice, sorcier the common term for the practitioner (magicien occurs in the late fifteenth century). L'enchanteur in the twelfth and thirteenth centuries "est exclusivement littéraire, poétique," while enchantement or enchanter designate the "song" or spells of a sorcier. (Wagner 26, 50, 139)

[6]See also Ricardo-Gil, The Practice of Witchcraft and Magic in Fact and Fiction During the French Middle Ages. Also, in the twelfth century, a magician/heretic Eude de L'Etoile and his followers had a retreat in Broceliande where they "perpetuated the ancient warfare between the Church and magic till death at the stake and in prison ended all." (N. K. Chadwick, "The Colonization" 299)

[7]The collection published in 1849 and 1877 by Lady Charlotte Guest inaccurately applies the term "mabinogi" to all the tales she translated. Critics now agree that only Pwyll, Branwen, Manawydan, and Math are the Mabinogi proper. See Bromwich, "Character of the Early Welsh Tradition," 101.

[8]Pedeir Keinc y Mabinogi 70. Subsequently cited in the text as PKM.

[9]The Mabinogi and Other Medieval Welsh Tales, ed. and tr. by Patrick L. Ford, 103. Subsequently cited in the text as Ford.

[10]Welsh dieties were also envisioned as maintaining courts, retinues, and families; the deities, "being more strictly supernatural magicians," required magic for their own continuance. (Powell 127)

[11]The word manawyd in Old Welsh designates a shoemaker's awl, further indicating his connection with the triad.

[12]Gorssed Arberth--The Mound of Arberth--is also where Pwyll first sees Rhiannon (PKM 9). One of the courtiers tells Pwyll, "kynnedyf yr orssed yw, pa dylydauc bynnac a eistedo arnei, nat a odyno heb un o'r deupeth, ay kymriw neu archolleu, neu ynteu a welei rywedawt." (PKM 9). "It is a characteristic of the mound that any noble who sits upon it shall not leave it without the one of two things: either he will be wounded or suffer an injury, or he will see a marvel." (Ford 42).

[13]"Pwyll" is used in early poetry to mean wisdom or good sense, which is also Manawydan's outstanding virtue. (McKenna 39)

[14] Until the twelfth century, medieval heresy was restricted to the Continent; the Celtic church kept itself isolated, and England had a chain of outside threats (pagan) to deal with until the eleventh century. The first English heresy appears in the twelfth century (Russell, Dissent and Reform 245). It is unlikely that heresies would have affected any of the saints' lives, or secular tales, discussed here in such a way as to make the "magic" in them questionably foreign.

[15]Vitae Sanctorum Britanniae et Genealogiae, ed. A. W. Wade-Evans, 144. Subsequently cited as VSB in the text.

[16]See Thompson 85-87.

[17]Peter Brown, in "Sorcery, Demons and the Rise of Christianity," notes that the main difference between the saint and the sorcerer is that the saint has a kind of "vested" power, while the sorcerer's technique is "unreliable and, above all, cumbersome" (140). Keith Thomas, however, spells out the difference as follows: "This belief that earthly events could be influenced by supernatural intervention was not in itself a magical one. For the essential difference between the prayers of a churchman and the spells of a magician was that only the latter claimed to work automatically; a prayer had no certainty of success and could not be granted if God chose not to concede it. A spell, on the other hand, need never go wrong, unless some detail of ritual observance had been omitted or a rival magician had been practising stronger counter-magic" (41).

[18]See also note to ll. 1989ff. (309).

[19]See "De Chophur in da Muccida," one of the *remscéla*, or "foe tales."

[20]The earliest surviving version is from the mid-sixteenth century, but the story undoubtedly dates from earlier (Ford, 159).

[21]*Vitae Sanctorum Hiberniae*, ed. Charles Plummer, 240. Subsequently cited in the text as VSH. A note on the dates of some saints and their lives:

	Flourished	Ms. Date
Coemgen	7th c.	14th c.
Abban	6/7th c.	14th c.
Brendan	6th c.	14th c.
Aed	6th c.	14th c.
Molasius	6th c.	16th c.

Both the text of the *Táin* and of "The Battle of Magh mucramha" are taken from the 12th-century Book of Leinster. In all these cases, there is evidence that the narratives existed much earlier than these mss., often 9th or 10th century, and for the sake of argument I am here accepting that evidence.

[22]Ritual cursing as a means of bringing down divine wrath is reported in Britain in the times of Roman conquest. See Piggott 116.

[23]"Life of St. Mochuda of Lismore," in *Life of St. Declan of Ardmore and Life of St. Mochuda of Lismore*, ed. and tr. by P. Power, 127. Subsequently cited as Power in the text.

[24]"Saint" in the pan-Brittonic world designates a "holy person" rather than only canonized saints, but still seems inconsistent with secular duties. See Lagorio, "Pan-Brittonic Hagiography," 34.

[25]Gwynllyw's *Vita* says he handed over the kingdom to Cadog; the *Vita Sancti Cadoci*, however, notes the father's death as a religious but says nothing about Cadog ruling after or for his father at any time.

[26]See Bloomfield 113.

[27]The text from Tours, "[Chap. IX] [de sortilegiis]. . . ne aliquis, vel aliqua, sortilegium exercere praesumat--Si quis uero sortilegii crimen repertus fuerit. . . ." From Trèves, "[Chap. 37]. . . conjurationes quae fiunt per inspectionem ignis, uel gladii seu alio quovis modo. . ." (on divination) (Wagner 100).

[28]"Christianus qui occiderit aut fornicationem fecerit aut more gentilium ad aruspicem iurauerit, per singula cremina annum penitentiae agat; . . . qui crediderit esse lamiam in saeculo, quae interpraetatur striga . . . nec ante in ecclesiam recipiendus quam ut idem creminis quod fecit sua iterum uoce reuocat . . . " (Bieler 56). See also 78-80, 100, and 104.

Chapter Two

Merlin the Prophet: Geoffrey of Monmouth's *Historia*

When Merlin is introduced for the first time by Geoffrey of Monmouth in the *Historia Regum Britanniae* (HRB), he is clothed in motifs which he will never shed. Geoffrey creates (or perhaps perpetuates from lost narratives) what we now recognize as the world of Arthurian history and pre-history, and he establishes Merlin's basic role in relation to that world. The HRB encompasses almost 2,000 years of British history, but Merlin's role, while one among many, is far from minor.[1] Unlike the HRB, Geoffrey's other work, the *Vita Merlini* (VM), discussed in the next chapter, takes an individualistic, pseudo-biographical approach. Here Merlin is the major character. Neither of these two narratives is romance, although each contains "romance elements" which were appropriated and expanded upon in later writing. Each narrative does, however, lay an implicit claim by reason of genre to being non-fiction--the HRB as history, the VM as "life"--and neither is truly what it purports to be. Geoffrey uses each genre and its conventions to his own ends in each work, presuming, I think, that his reader has an acquaintance with both historical and hagiographical writings to help in understanding his narratives.

In leading up to a discussion of the *Historia*, Robert Hanning in *The Vision of History in Early Britain* explores the development of the Christian view and practice of historical writing which medieval British historians inherited and used in their treatments of the island's history. The methods of Eusebius and Orosius dominated the early historical works, in which the historical order parallels the divine, and the Christian can "find the footprints of God in history" by applying the methods of scriptural exegesis to historical events (Hanning, Vision, 26, 36). Divine judgement is continually at work, and biblical patterns point the way to interpreting later historical events. There is no minute search into causal connections, since what happens is determined by God (Milburn 71). In addition, the battle between Christ and the devil can be seen through the history of the Church and Christian peoples (Hanning, Vision, 26; Milburn 70).

Augustine's view of history takes into account the individual actions of people; while still seeing history with a "divinely ordained end," the movement to that end happens as an accretion of personal choices and the development of a uniquely Christian personality (Hanning, Vision, 35). Augustine reaffirms that God does control history; fortune or blind chance does not fit into Augustine's (or Eusebius') views (Milburn 78). Orosius combines Eusebian and Augustinian ideas, creating his own "synthesis of national history and biblical narrative with its exegetical interpretation" (Hanning, Vision, 42). Subsequent continental historians continue to use these historical methods (Gregory of Tours and Paul the Deacon are major exemplars), and history continued to be explicitly didactic.

Such a view of history was perpetuated in Britain with more or less success until the advent of Norman rule. With the new order,

Hanning sees a new approach to history. While still loyal to the Orosian method, the Anglo-Norman historians (William of Malmesbury, Orderic Vitalis, and Henry of Huntingdon in particular) move away from the focus on society which Eusebius and Orosius preferred, and begin instead to focus more on individuals. Where earlier historians might have concerned themselves with the characteristics of a king which would fit him into the mold of Ideal Christian Monarch, the Anglo-Normans sought to separate kings from one another by detailed portraits of character which would make each a unique individual and help to explain some characteristics of his reign (Hanning, _Vision_, 131).[2]

With particular reference to what would become known as the Arthurian epoch, Geoffrey's contemporaries William and Henry tried to formulate a full account of both British and Saxon events, but the Latin sources they used, Bede and the Anglo-Saxon Chronicle, understandably gave very little of the British point of view. Earlier British history, too, had to be pieced together from Roman materials. Henry of Huntingdon tried to hunt down enough verifiable information on the Britons to include in his _Historia Anglorum_, but was unsuccessful--hence his excitement when, later, Geoffrey's _Historia_ was handed to him on a visit to Normandy (Leckie 38-39).

Geoffrey of Monmouth enters the revised arena of Anglo-Norman historical writing and goes one step further (leaving aside his active imagination). Where Henry, for example, selected those kings for highest praise "who renounce their kingdoms and join monasteries or travel to Rome," Geoffrey's "kings are more or less successful depending on their ability to hold the kingdom together, govern it well, and expand it if possible" (Rosenhaus 36). The HRB scrupulously avoids any direct scriptural interpretation of events and, Hanning argues, presents a very secular view of history (Vision 171-72). While I would not go as far as Hanning does in declaring the HRB totally free of the Christian view of history, the pure exegetical method is not present, and divine judgement is brought into play very sparingly, only at crucial junctures. Rosenhaus, too, sees Geoffrey not diverging from his contemporaries, but rather representative of them in his "attempt to reconcile divergent causalities" (180).

Geoffrey uses the Bible as a history book to set events in relative time, but he uses Roman history the same way. The narrative provides its own standards for drawing moral lessons, but these standards are not entirely lacking in Christian bases. However, the preference Geoffrey shows for using non-Christian prophets like the Sibyl and Merlin instead of saints (as, for example, we find in William of Malmesbury) further secularizes the work, and ecclesiastical history, even as it might relate to political affairs, is barely in evidence. In all, Geoffrey's emphasis is clearly on the actions of people, not of God, in history, though the line drawn between them is rather fine.

Critics have had problems with several aspects of Geoffrey's narrative, and I cannot deal with all of them here even were they relevant to the figure of Merlin. One puzzle, however, demands attention--the prophecies of Merlin. Not only is there debate as to whether the whole of Book VII, acknowledged as an earlier, independent work, belongs in the HRB at all, but there is also the inconsistency between Merlin's various prophecies (in and out of Book VII) and what actually happens to the British. I find myself convinced that Book VII does belong, and therefore argue with that assumption.[3] The inconsistencies have received less attention, and the remainder of this chapter will attempt to deal with that particular problem as it relates to the portrayal of Merlin. I am especially intrigued that, although Robert de Boron, among others, responded creatively to the intimations of Antichrist in Geoffrey's portrayal of Merlin in the Historia, modern critics have done little with this aspect of Merlin in reading the problematical latter half of the work.

In the prophecy to Vortigern, Merlin says that six generations of the family of "The Boar of Cornwall" (usually taken to be Arthur) will follow on the throne, but Arthur dies without issue; the crown passes to the Duke of Cornwall's son. In a later prophecy to Uther, Merlin states that Uther's daughter, Arthur's sister, will produce the subsequent line of British kings. The sister, however, is never married to the Duke of Cornwall.[4] The sister's son we know of, Mordred, is killed after usurping the throne, and his sons killed soon after. And even if the Duke of Cornwall's son were somehow Arthur's nephew, the next king after him wipes out that line, too. No six generations no matter how hard we try. Merlin also foretells a glorious future for the British, but as it happens this glory is short-lived and is followed by their rapid descent into obscurity.

I wish to examine some problems of interpretation created by Merlin's unfulfilled prophecies and propose a reading which takes them into account.

The pattern of the rise and fall of British monarchs in the *Historia* builds to a climax in Books IX and X with the reign of Arthur; his rule is given the most space and it is detailed proportionately. Merlin, however, appears earlier, in the center of the work, Books VI, VII, and VIII. His first appearance comes at a low point in Britain's history, when the lust and ambition of Vortigern brought about an influx of Saxons, who now have turned on him. Vortigern is desperate for a course of action against the threats of Hengist, and his seers advise him to build a defensive tower in Wales. When the walls continually collapse in construction, these men tell the king to find a "iuvenum sine patre" and strengthen the mortar with his blood. The boy is found, Merlin, but not only does Merlin know more than Vortigern's seers about the cause of the falling walls, he also prophesies the future history of Britain, including the imminent death of Vortigern himself.[5]

A mood of expectation surrounds this section. Vortigern has essentially abandoned his realm to the Saxons, having fled after giving in to Hengist's latest demands. The interruption of the action with the book of Merlin's prophecies stops us at a crucial point, when Vortigern's fate and that of Britain are unclear. Merlin's prophecies announce that the height of Britain's glory is yet ahead[6]--the nation's fortunes will once again rise--and the reestablishment of the legitimate line will bring about this glorious era.

By using Merlin with his supernatural birth and powers to guide Britain into its height, Geoffrey seems to place the primary responsibility for events above the human plane, though he generally eschews the supernatural. But Merlin is no Christian saint here. If anything, his birth reeks of demonic origins; this "odor" cannot be ignored when we look at the significance of Merlin's birth. When brought before Vortigern, Merlin's mother explains that a mysterious nocturnal visitor from the spirit world had intercourse with her, resulting in Merlin. The motif of the *incubus daemonum* furnishes a rich fund of speculation and development in later literature, but Geoffrey at first seems to make little of the incubus motif except as a solution to the riddle of the "boy without a father" posed by Vortigern's seers.

One can perceive a larger purpose, perhaps, when Geoffrey's version is compared with the parallel section in the earlier *Historia Brittonum*. There, the boy found for Vortigern (named Ambrosius) is given no demonic origin, and is in fact revealed to be the son of a Roman emperor.[7] Vortigern looks foolish for believing the pagan magicians' claims, and the presence of St. Germanus railing against Vortigern's alliance with heathens reinforces the moral intent. Geoffrey, however, leaves out St. Germanus, adds the motif of the demon birth and does not unravel the mystery by revealing an earthly father. Merlin is firmly out of the ordinary, the pagans are dismissed as liars, and Vortigern even retains some of his dignity.

Merlin's birth could be seen, following Paul Zumthor's view, as a possible "post-figuration" of Christ (Zumthor, Merlin, 14), like Ambrosius' birth in the Historia Brittonum. Such a reading, however, must dismiss the mother's story and Maugan's confirmation of it and leave Merlin's paternity unknown. Zumthor sees Geoffrey downplaying the miraculous elements of his predecessors in most situations, as indeed he does. But Zumthor goes on to note that, "l'élément merveilleux soit d'ordre plus intérieur, quasi-surnaturel, et réside exclusivement dans le personnage même d'Ambrosius Merlinus et le message qu'il apporte" (Zumthor, Merlin, 26; my emphasis). We are still left, then, with the presence of Merlin's birth as a marvellous event and his unique prophetic gift.[8] Is the incubus just a face-saving explanation for an illegitimate birth, which still could lend Merlin a Christlike role such as a saint would fill? (Indeed the fatherless, even illegitimate, birth motif is common to saints' lives, as we have seen.[9]) This interpretation, giving Merlin a very positive character, has been traditional. But is it actually the daemonum part which should be emphasized in Merlin's paternity?

A twelfth-century reader could be expected to pick up the intimations of Antichrist in Geoffrey's Merlin. Medieval legend connects Antichrist closely with the devil (often, but not always, giving him a demon father), whose primary goal is to lead Christians into apostasy. The devil possesses and instructs Antichrist, providing him with "powers of deception and wonder making"; also, discord in society will precede his birth (Emmerson 76, 215). He will either be a tyrannical king or claim to be Christ in His second coming, or both. Merlin here does not, of course, fulfill all aspects of this role, but as a "type" of Antichrist, he does have both the demonic connection and powers of deception. He is also born amidst social turmoil, when Vortigern removes the monk Constans from his cloister to be king.

Concerning incubi, as early as Philo[10] (first century AD), fallen angels were allowed the power of impregnating women; the offspring need not be evil, however. Isidore classed incubi with other demons (demoted pagan gods) of the classical era and believed them capable of intercourse. The common sources for information on incubi--Isidore, Augustine, Gregory and Jerome--were all available in England from at least the eighth century (Kiessling 10-14 passim).

Influenced by these sources, Geoffrey's contemporaries saw the incubus' son Merlin in demonic terms. Reacting to the <u>Historia</u>, John of Salisbury implies that Merlin was inspired by a demonic spirit (Zumthor, <u>Merlin</u>, 93), and William of Newburgh "attributes Merlin's prophetic powers to his incubus father" (Curley 221).[11] Robert de Boron expanded upon the implications, building a background of diabolic plotting as a prelude to Merlin's birth, which is, in Robert's work and its continuations, actually intended to be the birth of Antichrist, and Robert goes to great lengths to convince the reader that his Merlin, while demonic by paternity, is a legitimate, baptized, servant of God in his narrative. The author of the prose Lancelot will prefer to leave Merlin demonic to provide the Lady of the Lake with a legitimate reason for imprisoning him (see Chapter Four).

Alongside these views, we also have the Celtic traditions of "fairy" creatures, reflected in Walter Map's De Nugis Curialium and Marie de France's Lais. These Celtic creatures are not necessarily evil (cf. the angelic offspring in Philo), and some may even be good (Kiessling 43). Geoffrey may well have known these Celtic traditions and used them, but he would also have been aware of the traditional Christian (negative) views of such demon-like creatures, as described in Chapter One.

We have, then, two very different possibilities for interpreting Merlin's birth. First, we could follow the line found in the Historia Brittonum, and inject a condemnation of Vortigern and his pagan magicians for believing such a far-fetched tale as that which Merlin's mother pawns off on them. Here, the gullibility of the king reinforces his unfitness to rule; Merlin in spite of the tale is not demonic but still unique. Second, we can read it just as Geoffrey has left it--ambiguous, but with stated and confirmed demonic possibilities. In this case, we need to examine more fully the implications of this ambiguity for the narrative.

After his introduction in the Vortigern section, Merlin's next appearance in the text comes when Ambrosius, established on the throne, seeks to build a memorial to the British slain treacherously by Saxons on Salisbury plain. An archbishop suggests Merlin for the task, and Merlin obliges the king by transporting the famous Giants' Dance from Ireland, much to the amazement of all. Ambrosius is soon buried at Salisbury himself, and Uther is told of his descendants ruling the kingdom.

Because Ambrosius has left no son, his brother Uther succeeds him. Uther will not be childless, however--thanks to Merlin's help. Geoffrey does not make clear what, if anything, gives Merlin and/or Uther the right to pursue the illicit love Uther has for Igerne. Igerne is married, a Christian. If Merlin is not demonic, but instead God's tool, the trickery imposed upon Igerne takes on one coloration; if, however, Merlin is demonic, the affair should clearly be condemned and its product suspect. (Compare Mordred's adultery with Guenevere later, which Geoffrey also refuses to elaborate on.) Again, Geoffrey frustrates us by giving no clear directions to follow, but we must note that the child born from Uther's illicit night with Igerne, Arthur, could not have been born without Merlin's help. As indicated above, Merlin twice gives prophecies regarding Uther's offspring. One might expect some clues from Geoffrey in these prophecies, but here again we encounter difficulties; the clues are there, yes, but the prophecies are contradictory and neither is fulfilled.

So, has a demonic Merlin issued false prophecies about a demonic pawn? Or--yet another twist--do the irresponsible actions of the British people act to thwart legitimate prophecies?

Following this second possibility, the Britons reap what they sow throughout the *Historia*. Whenever civil strife divides the kingdom, disaster beckons. Invasions, tyrannical rule, and other catastrophic events ensue. When the realm is united and ruled well, the kingdom thrives. Wise rule, however, includes not only avoiding civil wars, but also avoiding personal ambition which causes the nation's interest to take second place.

Earlier in the Historia Maximian, in gaining the seat of the Roman Empire, denuded Britain of its fighting men in the process and opened the way for invaders. The examples of good and, here, bad rule throughout the Historia are generally straightforward. While Geoffrey does not condemn warfare or conquest per se, he is careful in distinguishing between negative and positive motives for either. As noted by Rosenhaus, "bravery plays a part both in the success of the kingdom and in its failure" (22).

The parallel of Brittany (Armorica) often offers a contrast to the island. These people, who settled in the wake of Conan and Maximian, often provide their relatives from Britain refuge, and sometimes even troops for help against invaders: Constantine, the father of Uther and Ambrosius, was brother to the Breton king (VI,4), and Cadwallo later receives help from Salomon (XII,8). Because they have not squandered their men on civil wars, the Bretons are in a position to help, as well as in a position to censure Britain's weakness. When the Breton Salomon laments the British inability to defend their land, Cadwallo blames Maximian for taking all the good men (i.e., Salomon's ancestors) with him, leaving the dregs for the island's defense. Although the characters, on occasion, can see the reasons for the failures of

British rule, the problem lies in the fact that as a people the British never reform, preferring to blame the past for their present problems.

As indicated above, Merlin's role in this historical pattern is ambiguous. Although subsequent works portray Merlin as an infallible prophet and friend to the three kings (Ambrosius, Uther, Arthur), such is not the case here. In fact, Merlin has no dealings with Arthur that we see, and he is shown to be wrong in several instances where his prophecy is very clearly expressed. The inconsistencies must have bothered at least one contemporary, Wace, since he changes the two sections to eliminate the problems.[12] While Merlin's skills as an engineer are well established by the transferral of Stonehenge to Salisbury, and his mastery of disguise by the trick used to smuggle Uther into Tintagel, Merlin's prophetic skills or gifts cannot be trusted so easily.

Even so, the prophecies which fill Book VII lend the figure of Merlin an importance which Geoffrey manipulates to cast the worst possible light first on Vortigern, then on the future kings who do not learn from history. The two kings who Merlin helps are, by Geoffrey's standards, worthy of aid; neither casts covetous eyes outside Britain, they are legitimate sons and successors, and they restore peace to the island. Whether the restraint of Ambrosius and Uther is due to their preoccupation with consolidating their victories, to their early deaths, or to their wisdom, it remains that Merlin helps them and he is absent when Arthur assumes the throne. While this legitimate aid may argue against a strongly demonic role for Merlin, it does point up distinct differences between the two brothers and their son and nephew as rulers which still cast a shadow over Arthur's actions.

Before his death by poison, Uther reigns in peace long enough (ca. fifteen years) for Arthur to mature before the Saxons renew their invasions. Uther's only sought-after war was that which toppled Vortigern and cast out the Saxons. Note that when Uther fights to remove the Giants' Dance from Ireland (VIII, 12), he does not attempt to take over Ireland. Arthur, however, is not satisfied with just reuniting Britain. He conquers Ireland and northern Europe, then when provoked by the Roman emperor (who is upset at losing Gaul), he sets off to war on the continent, leaving Britain in finally traitorous hands. However much glory foreign conquest adds to Arthur's reign, in the end it contributes directly to his fall. Nor does Britain ever again attain the "heights" it scaled under Arthur.

Arthur's initial ability to maintain unity in Britain inevitably leads the close reader of Geoffrey to wonder how long this luck will hold. Given the pattern of history which Geoffrey draws in the Historia, the civil war caused by Mordred's treason can only be expected. In pursuing the war against Rome, Arthur pursues personal ends, takes the prime fighting men to the continent, and, as before with Maximian, chaos fills the vacuum.

Unlike his father, Arthur conquers beyond the island's borders. His pride in his achievements is pictured clearly in his reaction to the fearful preparation of foreign kings against the possibility of a campaign: "Cumque id arturo notificatum esset extollens se quia cunctis timori erat. totam europam sibi subdere aflectat" (IX, 11; Griscom 446). When the challenge from Rome is later brought, he and his advisors do not hesitate to go to war but plunge in almost gleefully, reflecting the same spirit which led their ancestors in their fights and which Geoffrey condemns.[13]

Merlin's absence when Arthur's conquests begin, in the light of his former aid to Ambrosius and Uther, clues in the reader that a new cycle has begun, one without Merlin (in spite of the later, also problematical, vision of Cadwallader; see below). When he brought the Giants' Dance from Ireland for Ambrosius, Merlin made the point that the stones have healing qualities--symbolic, I think, of the healing that Ambrosius was then beginning in Britain after the devastations under Vortigern. But later Ambrosius, dead from a Saxon poisoner, is buried under the stone circle among the nobles earlier slain by Saxon treachery. Like Ambrosius, Uther becomes a victim of Saxon poison, but in spite of all this, the warning represented by the Dance seems to have limited meaning for Arthur. In his reign, the Saxons are soon under control, and the realm is unified. The possibility of treason from other than Saxons does not seem to occur to him, but the careful reader who remembers earlier episodes (most notably, and most recently, the betrayal of Constans by Vortigern)[14] knows better and, from the clues provided by Arthur's pride and ambition, can expect a decline for Arthur.

Starting with Arthur, Uther's descendants are the subject of Merlin's optimistic prophecies, but Merlin's demonic paternity casts doubt on the nature of his prophetic role in the Historia. At the most radical end, Merlin as demon could be expected to tell half-truths to his own perverted ends, perhaps even intending to bring about the eventual loss of Britain to the heathen Saxons. If so, the irony that the Saxons are Christian by the time they take over is further proof of God's ability to twist demonic purposes to His own ends. Since the nation never recovers after Arthur's war with Mordred, perhaps the fact that without Merlin Arthur would not have been born also takes on an ironic significance, Arthur's life in such a case being part of the demonic plan to deliver over Britain to the Saxons.

Although the characters in the Historia know of Merlin's questionable birth since it was revealed in Vortigern's court, they never raise or even think to raise any doubts concerning his motives.[15] Geoffrey seems to have made them deliberately blind to the possible traitor in their midst (just as Arthur is blind to possible treason by Mordred). Indeed, Merlin is instead extolled as a prophet extraordinaire, and his advice and help are regarded highly by the characters. And his similarity to both Samuel and Daniel lends a certain reliability to him, on the reader's part, as well.[16] Is Geoffrey playing with the reader? Are we actually supposed to overlook the demonic tale regarding his birth and take Merlin as the positive character his peers do? Are we supposed to question at all the mother's story as a possible cover-up for an earthly misbehavior? Although her corroborator, Maugan, is pagan and can be expected to believe such tales, his authority is

Apuleius, who is also St. Augustine's source for ideas about demons (*De civ.* 8-9).

Even if one cannot accept Merlin as a full-fledged demon (which I admittedly find difficult), the demonic undertones and the inconsistent prophecies, combined with the predominant character traits of the British, lead me to suspect that Geoffrey is underlining his portrait of the latter-day Britons as unworthy of the land by calling into question this way their most cherished era. Merlin is indeed wrong about the descendants of Arthur--this could lead one to question whether Arthur actually is the "Boar of Cornwall" Merlin earlier foretold or whether that prophecy, too, has gone astray. Arthur's legitimacy is questionable because of the adulterous trick played on Igerne--and Merlin made that trick possible. *Is* this the demon in Merlin carrying out infernal plans--or just the irony-loving demon in Geoffrey?

Up to Merlin's entrance, Geoffrey is a totally reliable narrator (if one accepts that he is writing a fabricated history). But, as Wayne Booth reminds us, a reliable narrator can come forth with irony, and the warning to the reader that irony is at play need not be direct. "Any grotesque disparity between word and word or word and deed will serve," he says. And in the absence of "unmistakeable clues," the reader will have trouble with this irony (*Rhetoric* 159, 316-318). The prophecies and inconsistencies, troublesome indeed, I think are Geoffrey's alternative, ironic, "voice." His political purpose, presenting the characteristics which contribute to a nation's fall, is strengthened by the ambiguities, inconsistencies, and doubts surrounding Merlin and Arthur, since they emphasize the flaws of the British people.

For one, they show that the British cannot recognize trouble even when it stares them in the face. As a people, the British have become increasingly ambitious and desirous of glory. Merlin prophesied glory for the British--thus, say the British, Merlin must be a true prophet. If he happens to be wrong about the way it will come about and the time, that is no reason to believe that it will never happen some way, some day. Merlin thus seems to be a true prophet, and the British want to believe him, but he is not. Their blind trust in Merlin mirrors their blindness to their own faults.

Second, unlike Maximian, Arthur at the beginning is a promising candidate for the title of Good King; he promotes peace on the island, provides for his men and family, and he is personally brave, generous, and a good leader. But he fails, ambition and pride his vices. Instead of returning home after defeating the Roman army under Lucius, for example, he winters over to prepare for a march on Rome itself. During this time, Mordred usurps the throne.

Whether Arthur is doomed to fail by demonic intervention, or whether he is the last hope of the British and fails because of their communal faults, once he is dead, the end comes quickly, in less than 150 years (during which time the Saxons become Christian). Geoffrey's irony works by blinding the British to this fact. Arthur's "glorious era" may be a climax, but his time is relatively short and the peace he brings fleeting. He reigns less than thirty years. Compare Geoffrey's praise for the long--and peaceful--reigns of Ebraucus, Dunvallo Molmutius, and Heli (all 40 years) and Leir (60 years). Other kings, too, are given more direct praise than Arthur: Lucius (IV,19-V,1), Dunvallo (II,17), and several others in passing. If Arthur is indeed the "best" Britain can produce, then no wonder God gives up; but I think Geoffrey's British may be misguided when they look to the reign of Arthur as their supreme product.

If Merlin's prophecies are not deliberately misleading, they are still only wishful thinking. (A tension exists between the two possibilities, one that Geoffrey leaves intact.) The prophesied line of succession then proves false simply because the behavior of the British (both king and people) does not allow it to come about. The inconsistency between the two prophecies underlines the doubt the reader should feel in their fulfillment, a doubt justified by later events. Instead of deliberate lies, perhaps Merlin presents to the British a picture of what might be--if they mend their ways.[17] However, the British people provide their own type of prophecy, through the pattern of their past behavior. The established cycle of rise and fall, of unity and civil strife, of expansion and invasion proves true to itself.

The advent of Arthur and the warning of Merlin's prophecies, then, can be seen as Britain's last chance, and in that event Merlin's role in determining what happens centers around pronouncing their goal and providing Arthur, even by adultery, for that last chance to reach it. Through no fault or virtue of Merlin, the people and their leader prove unworthy of the kingdom. The Sibyl's prophecy, in which Brutus is given the island and the promise of descendants who will rule the whole earth, is fulfilled well before Arthur comes onto the scene. Both Maximian and the first Constantine became Roman emperors, and even earlier Brennius ruled Rome as well.

Early in the first book, though, Geoffrey warns us that the British will lose their land: "donec ultione diuina propter ipsorum superbiam superueniente" (I, 2; Griscom 222). Arthur's pride, like Maximian's, leads Britain into dire straits. In addition, since Arthur failed in becoming Emperor where the two earlier succeeded, we have a good indication that Britain's end is near, that the decline has already begun.[18] The example of Arthur, promising at first, turns negative as personal ambition takes the place of national defense in Arthur's priorities.[19]

Let us look at one other supernatural intrusion for the sake of comparison. Near the end of Book XII, Cadwallader has taken refuge in Brittany and wants to lead a force to regain his lands, but it is too late. Cadwallader is warned away from Britain by an angelic voice: "intonuit ei vox angelica dum classem pararet. ut ceptis suis desisteret. Nolebat enim deus britones in insula britannie diutius regnare. & antequam tempus aduenisset quod merlinus arturo prophetauerat" (XII, 17; Griscom 533). Cadwallader goes to Rome and dies among the elect of God, his "faithfulness" rewarded. However, the final emphasis is laid not on the prophecy of regaining the kingdom, but on the Britons' inability to unify and keep peace. The Britons are pushed to the far ends of the island, and

> Degenerati autem a britannica nobilitate gualenses. numquam postea monarchiam insulae recuperauerunt. immo nunc sibi, interdum saxonibus ingrati consurgentes externas ac domesticas clades incessanter agebant. (Griscom, pp. 535-536)

They still fight among themselves, and they have been demoted linguistically as well as politically: Britons no longer, but Welsh, their chances are up. For the British, however, it is important to notice that they believe Merlin's prophecy of glory right up to, and beyond, the point where God denies them sovereignty, as indicated by Cadwallader's vision.

Now let us return to that <u>vox angelica</u>. It said, "quod merlinus arturo prophetauerat." Here is another inconsistency: we never see Merlin with Arthur (he disappears after the night Arthur is conceived), and we never see this prophecy.[20] Has Geoffrey (again?) left something out? Has the angel made a mistake? All this inconsistency leads one to distrust any supernatural voice, angelic, demonic or ambiguous, and look to other voices in the narrative for direction. The facts, and the criticisms from Geoffrey himself, focus on the bellicose nature of the Britons and their pride. Geoffrey lashes out at them in Book XI:

> Quid ociosa gens pondere inmanium scelerum oppressa. quid semper ciuilia prelia siciens tete domesticis in tantum debilitasti motibus. que cum prius longe posita regna potestati tue subdidisses. nunc uelut bona uinea degenerata in amaritudinem uersa. patriam. coniuges. liberos nequeas ab inimicis tueri? Age ergo age ciuile discidium. parum intelligens illud euangelicum. Omne regnum in se ipsum diuisum desolabitur. & domus supra domum cadet. Quia ergo regnum tuum in se diuisum fuit. quia furor ciuilis discordie. & liuoris fumus mentem tuam hebetauit. quia superbia tua uni regi obedientiam ferre te non permisit. cernis iccirco patriam tuam ab impiissimis paganis desolatam. domus etiam eiusdem

> supra domos reuersas. quod posteri tui in futurum lugebunt. Uidebunt etenim barbare leene catulos opida. ciuitates atque ceteras eorundem possessiones obtinere. ex quibus misere expulsi prioris dignitatis statum uel uix uel nunquam recuperabunt. (XI,9; Griscom, 505-506)

At this point in the narrative, the British are doomed to lose their sovereignty, and Geoffrey here makes sure we know why, echoing his comments in Book I. Geoffrey as narrator rarely intrudes his voice into the text (indeed less often than one might wish given the problems with the work), so when he does intrude we need to pay close attention. In the same way, I think, the rare supernatural intrusions need to be given close attention, perhaps as reflections of Geoffrey's own voice in ironic disguise. Both point to the national character flaws which result in the Britons' fall.

The irony seems more apparent if we juxtapose a few passages in the HRB with their parallels in Virgil's _Aeneid_, one of Geoffrey's obvious sources. Compare Merlin's prophecies to Vortigern to Aeneas' vision of the future in the Underworld in Book VI. Aeneas' prophecy is presented to him by his father's shade and serves to give him a necessary push toward fulfilling his own and Rome's destiny. Aeneas' fortunes are on the way up. Vortigern's luck has run out. Merlin's prophecy foretells death for the king, the reestablishment of his enemies on the throne, and the coming of a Golden Age after his death. In addition, while Rome's history under the exiled Trojans is about to begin, Britain's under the British is nearing its end: the prophecy in each work signals a clear turning point, positive for the _Aeneid_ and negative for the HRB.

A second comparison juxtaposes Aeneas, who at the end has conquered his new kingdom, and Cadwallader, who has abandoned Britain at the angel's directive to conquer his "new kingdom," heaven. Similarly, within the HRB, the exile of Brutus, Aeneas' grandson, at the beginning, full of eagerness seeking his new, promised land, gives a sharp contrast to Cadwallader's exile of abandonment. No longer is the conqueror the representative of the British, no longer Brutus, but Cadwallader the pilgrim. As pilgrim, Cadwallader is the "correct" representative of his people at the end of the HRB; he lives a holy life, rejecting worldly ambition, and Geoffrey clearly approves (XII, 18). The British people, however, have no repentance. They continue to fight among themselves, as well as occasionally against the Saxons. The vengeance of God against this unrepentant people is to deprive them of sovereignty. The Saxons, now Christian, have become the chosen people for this island.

Whether the British people reached their nadir purely on their own demerits; whether Merlin as demon worked to bring about their fall; or whether the British meet with divine vengeance for their bellicose nature and blindness born of pride, or even a combination of these, the result is the same. Merlin's prophecies, whatever other purpose they have, serve to deepen the sense of loss at the end. The fall was interrupted, hope again raised, only to be finally lost. The possibility that Arthur could have succeeded, that Merlin's prophecies regarding an orderly line of succession and Golden Age could come true remains in the realm of "might have been." The failure of the first prophecy lends doubt, too, to the equally problematic angelic vision of Cadwallader. If the blindly optimistic British wait for the time about which "Merlin prophesied to Arthur" to regain their land, they will wait a long time.

By the time he finished the HRB, Geoffrey may well have had similar doubts about the Normans in Britain. The promise of Henry I's reign was swept away by his death without an heir in 1135. The resultant chaos undid all progress begun in Wales and in the general reorganization through the kingdom. The civil wars divided the nobility, wreaked havoc on the land, and made life insecure for all (Nelson 172-73). Rather than a Golden Age under a new Arthur, Geoffrey may well have seen the coming fall of the Normans, a new cycle of chaos. He could easily have looked forward to the peaceful, eremetic life he next provides Merlin.

Notes - Chapter Two

[1]The question of historical veracity, or lack thereof, in the HRB will not be treated here. The work shall be viewed as a piece of literature, not history, and the standards of the two are, of course, different.

[2]See also Pähler 53-59.

[3]The lengthy prophecies in Book VII are meant to be somewhat obscure references, in part to Geoffrey's own period, in part to the future apocalypse. Lewis Thorpe is one who ascribes to the view that they are interpolated. I tend rather to agree with Pähler and others that the prophecy section and the history mesh and play off one another to heighten the overall meaning of the narrative. (See Thorpe 25 and Pähler 132-35). Several critics have worked to unravel the prophecies, among them J.S.P. Tatlock (see his Chapter 17) and Ed. Faral (54-65). I give Faral's outline as an example (he refers to his own chapter numbers; I include Griscom's parallel passages):

1. Events of HRB to Saxon victory: Ch. 112, ll. 1-37 (Griscom, p. 385, l. 5-p. 386, l. 11)
2. Saxon victory to Henry I: Ch. 112, l. 38-Ch. 113, l. 22 (Griscom, p. 386, l. 11-p. 387, l. 12)
3. Obscure references to Henry I's reign: Ch. 113, l. 23-end 113 (Griscom, p. 387, ll. 13-17)
4. Norman rule to end; Britons will regain independence with Breton help: Ch. 114-115 (Griscom, p. 387, l. 18-p. 390, l. 2)
5. Misc. catastrophes, ending with traditional signs of the Last Judgement: Ch. 116-117 (Griscom, p. 390, l. 3-p. 397).

As Pähler notes, not all the elements in Book VII are clear, nor is it in the nature of prophecies to be crystal-clear, either (136).

[4]<u>Historia</u> VIII, 21, she marries Loth; IX, 2, she marries Budicius. Lewis Thorpe suggests that for the latter marriage, one should read "Aurelius Ambrosius' sister" instead of "Arthur's sister," but he gives no manuscript evidence here to support it. (214, note 1).

[5]Were this "real" history, I would conjecture that Merlin was bold enough to tell the king what his clerks were afraid to reveal to him--cf. the comment at the beginning of Book VII: "Neminem enim presens etas produxerat qui ora sua in hunc modum coram ipso soluisset," (Griscom 398) at which point Vortigern asks, and Merlin reveals, what the king's own end will be. All HRB quotations are from Acton Griscom's edition.

[6]Geoffrey continues to present the British in control of the country until after the death of Arthur; most historians of the time placed the disintegration of British rule at the arrival of Hengist (Leckie 58). Clearly, that would not fit Geoffrey's needs in the HRB.

[7]*Historia Brittonum*, Chapters 41-42.

[8]It is not clear that Merlin uses magic in the HRB; his feats are amazing, yes, but Geoffrey refers to Merlin as an engineer (one skillful with mechanical things) in reference to Stonehenge, and he uses "drugs" at Tintagel (*medicaminibus*). I tend to agree with Tatlock, who comments, "The *flat truth* is that Geoffrey's Merlin is not a magician" (364).

[9]See also Pähler, 155. William of Auvergne (ca. 1180-1249), however, theorizes that the demon collects sperm as succubus and gets rid of it as incubus, so Merlin would technically be human, not demon (Kiessling 25).

[10]The apocryphal Book of Tobit (2nd c. BC) also contains the story of a resident incubus, but it makes no comment on the possible offspring's nature.

[11]Curley examines the reactions of several contemporaries of Geoffrey to the prophecies. William of Newburgh, who had no love for the *Historia*, criticized the prophecies as being untrue at the same time that he attacked Geoffrey for presenting fable as fact; others disagreed with William over the truth of the prophecies. It is interesting, too, that William distinguishes between "demonic conjecture, which is often proved erroneous by later events" (viz. Merlin's prophecies which don't prove true) and actual foreknowledge, not only in connection with the *Historia*'s truthfulness, but also with Merlin's possible lack of truthfulness. As noted above, William attributes Merlin's powers to the demon father (221).

[12]The sections from Wace read as follows:

Dunc dist Merlin les prophecies
Que vus aves, co crei oies,
Des reis ki a venir esteint,
Ki la terre tenir deveient.
Ne vuil sun livre translater
Quant jo nel sai interpreter;
Nule rien dire ne vuldreie
Que si ne fust com jo dirreie.
Li reis ad mult loe Merlin
E mult le tint a buen devin;
Demanda li quant il murreit
E par quel mort il finereit,

Kar de sa fin ert en effrei.
"Guarde tei, dist il, guarde tei
Del feu as enfanz Constentin,
Kar par lur feu vendras a fin. (ll. 7535-7550)

(original prophecy to Vortigern)

Aureles primes rei sera
E par puisum primes murra.
Uther, sis freres, Pendragon,
Tendra empres la regiun;
Mais trop tost serra engrotez
E par tes eirs envenimez.
Sis filz, ki iert de Cornoaille,
Cume senglers fiers en bataille,
Le traiturs devurera
E tuz tes parens destruira;
Cil sera mult vaillans e prus,
Ses enemis conquerra tuz."
Merlin sa parole fina,
E Vortiger d'illuec turna. (ll. 7571-7584)

Li signes ki fu del dragun
Nus fist significatiun
De tei ki ies pruz e hardiz;
Li uns des rais, co est uns fiz
Que tu avras, de grant puissance,
Ki conquerra jesqu'ultre France;
Par l'altre rai, ki ca turna
E en set rais se devisa,
T'est une fille demustree,
Ki vers Escoce ert mariee.
Plusur bon eir de li naistrunt
Qui mers e terres conquerunt. (ll. 8333-8344)

(Merlin's prophecy to Uther)

Une voiz divine lui dist
Laissast cel eire, altre en preist;
L'eire d'Engleterre laissast,
A l'apostoile a Rome alast;
Ses pechiez iluec pardonez,
Ireit od les beneurez.
Engleis Bretaine aver deveient;
Ja Bretun n'i recuvereient
Jesqu'al tens que la prophecie
Que Merlin dist seit acumplie;
Ne ja co estre ne purreit
Desi la que li tens vendreit
Que les reliques de sun cors,
De sepulture traites fors,
Serreient de Rome aportees
E en Bretaine presentee. (ll. 14785-14800)

(*vox angelica* to Cadwallader)

The corresponding passages in Layamon are:

Original prophecy: ll. 7988-8042
To Uther: ll. 8962-8977
Vox angelica: ll. 16007-16028

(From the Caligula manuscript in Layamon: Brut.)

[13]When the challenge from Rome comes, Cador mentions a peaceful span of five years (IX, 15; Griscom 461). There may be some confusion, since earlier (IX,10) there was mentioned twelve years of peace after Arthur's initial, domestic, wars. The European conquests were then detailed, followed immediately by the gathering at which the Roman challenge is brought. In Wace, there is a greater emphasis on the twelve years of peace, since that is when the Round Table is founded. See Lacy, "The Form of the Brut's Arthurian Sequence," 155.

[14]Other examples of internal betrayal are those of Bassianus by Carausius (V, 3) and of Leir by his daughters and sons-in-law (II, 12-13).

[15]See the archbishop's recommendation of Merlin to Ambrosius in VIII, 10 (Griscom 409), for example.

[16]For a detailed comparison of the prophets, see Schwartz 42.

[17]Merlin's prophecies in Book VII do, however, reinforce the theme of disunity and disloyalty which will lead to the apocalypse (Pähler 137). These rather general prophecies are less of a problem than the specific ones.

[18]See Roberts, "Geoffrey of Monmouth and Welsh Historical Tradition," 37.

[19]While I do not agree with her argument in all its details, Rosenhaus' emphasis on the motif of superbia in the HRB is compelling. For the argument concerning Arthur and superbia see her Chapter Five, especially 226-43.

[20]For a fuller discussion of the problems, both in terms of the Griscom text and in general, inherent in the Vox Angelica prophecy, see Rosenhaus 181-85 and 196.

Chapter Three

Merlin Beatified: The *Vita Merlini*

With respect to later Arthurian literature, the *Vita Merlini* (VM), written approximately ten to fifteen years after the HRB, has negligible importance. But although the contents are relatively obscure, the attitudes and portraits the work reveals are significant. The overview of Celtic *vitae* in Chapter I gives a basic grounding in the type of local tradition Geoffrey might have known, and the VM can be treated (as the title invites, whether of Geoffrey's concoction or not) essentially as a "secular saint's life." The Norman period would later produce other secular, if somewhat fictionalized, lives of prominent men, such as that of William Marshall, Earl of Pembroke.[1] The VM, however, is a unique piece, treating material garnered from the saints' life tradition together with secular tradition; the technique is (perhaps not surprisingly) much like that of the HRB, with its combination of legitimate sources and authorial imagination to create a new type of work.

Like a saint's life, the VM is very episodic, with little progression other than chronological--in fact, the VM has more tightness to it than many saints' lives. The three major episodes may seem merely juxtaposed rather than connected, as Paul Zumthor sees them (*Merlin*, 37), but when compared to a saint's life, the VM possesses a remarkable unity. In the first episode, we see Merlin, maddened after losing three brothers in battle, restored to sanity and brought back to the court; he is unhappy there and eventually wins his release through his prescience. The second section centers around Taliesin's visit and learned conversations with Merlin. Finally, in a short episode, Merlin helps to cure another's madness and retires from prophecy. Basically, everything in the piece has a logical order, unlike many episodes retold in saints' lives which could be rearranged without great damage being done to the organization.

Geoffrey explicitly identifies the VM Merlin with the HRB Merlin, and in so doing interconnects the works by implication. To an extent, Geoffrey seems to aim at clearing up confusions in the HRB. Arthur has gone to Avalon already in the VM,[2] so it is chronologically possible (since Merlin is still alive) that Merlin could have given a prophecy to Arthur; also, the essence of that prophecy referred to by the angelic voice in HRB XII is here given (ll. 964-975). Then, the Duke of Cornwall's son Constantine is described as Arthur's nephew, so the prophecy regarding the sister's line is, but only in part, fulfilled. (Conan still kills Constantine and wipes out the legitimate, Arthurian, line.) These items, a recitation of the HRB Arthurian history by Merlin, and some sections of repeated prophecy, plus the tone with regard to British conduct, serve to connect the two works. The tone is probably the strongest link, since it plays an important role in each work.

The VM's first section acquaints us with the Celtic "Wild Man of the Woods" figure.[3] After going mad with grief, Merlin runs off to the woods alone and lives there for a time. A messenger from court finally locates him, calms him with music, and leads him back to court. However, Merlin is disturbed by the crowds and longs for his forest solitude. When King Rodarchus cannot persuade Merlin to stay, he orders the prophet (for Merlin is referred to as *vates* throughout) chained and guarded.

Merlin's chance for freedom comes when his sister (Ganieda, Rodarchus' queen) comes in with a leaf in her hair. To everyone's surprise, the sullen Merlin laughs. When the king presses him for an explanation, Merlin bargains for and wins release.[4] Merlin's mind is set on the *vita silvestris*, and he totally rejects all duties to the world at large. He will not resume ruling his own lands (he is *rex* as well as *vates*), nor will he maintain his wedded state. These things he now sees as superfluous, even inhibiting.

> Qui nemus ingressus fuerat rituque ferino
> vivebat, paciens concrete frigoris alge
> sub nive sub pluvia sub iniquo flamine venti,
> idque placebat ei pocius quam jura per urbes
> exercere suas gentesque domare feroces. (ll. 416-20)

A few years pass, and Merlin's skills with reading the stars tell him that his wife is remarrying, and that Conan has killed and succeeded Constantine as king of the Britons. Merlin gathers a herd of wild deer and goats for a wedding gift.[5]

The king's men again capture Merlin and he is kept at court, surly and unhappy. When he is taken on a walk in the marketplace, Merlin laughs at two sights; the king is told, and

> Ocius ergo volens Rodarchus scire quid esset
> quod portendisset risu, dissolvere nexus
> ilico jussit ei concedens posse reverti
> ad solitas silvas si risus exposuisset. (ll. 503-506)

Merlin's explanations reveal his amazing knowledge again, a buried treasure beneath a beggar and a man with new shoes now drowned (ll. 508-22). Again rejecting his sister's pleas to stay, Merlin leaves, but first tells her he will accept a house in the woods for a winter retreat and gives her specific directions as to its structure (ll. 551-61). This section ends with a repetition of the Vortigern prophecies (ll. 580-680) and Ganieda's lament at Rodarchus' death.

This first part gives a history of the adult Merlin and explains his forest retirement. Geoffrey has worked from several traceable sources to build his picture, among them the Life of St. Kentigern (or Lailoken tale) and the Welsh poems "Afallennau" and "Hoianau;" others will come into use later in the poem.[6] The pastoral element contrasted with the court emphasizes the extremity of Merlin's decision; we see what he is leaving behind. Although he is mad at first, Merlin quite deliberately chooses to return to the woods, making it clear that the forest supplies a need in him that civilization does not (however, in the third section, it is implied that Merlin has not at the current time fully regained his senses). Wars--to which he lost three brothers--, crowds, and regnal responsibilities are inferior to the peace, the solitude in nature, and the chance to scan the stars unimpeded. The opening lines of the recounted prophecy underscore the theme he (and Geoffrey) spoke in the HRB:

> O rabiem Britonum, quos copia diviciarum
> usque superveniens ultra quam debeat effert!
> Nolunt pace frui, stimulis agitantur Herinis.
> Civiles acies cognataque prelia miscent. (ll. 580-83)

He is tired of war and disgusted with the British people, especially the Welsh (ll. 601-2), so he draws himself apart to concentrate on more universal matters without distractions.

The Celtic saint, too, is prone to be a hermit or monk, drawn apart from society, spending his efforts in contemplation of God's world and in his personal spiritual growth. Early in the VM, we see an implicit Christian view attributed to Merlin in his plaint to Christ over the coming of winter (ll. 87ff.), and the portrait of Merlin in the VM continues to be more clearly within the borders of Christianity than in the HRB. The house which Ganieda builds for him, complete with servants and scribes, is not quite a secular monastery, but neither is it the solitary hermit's hovel. Merlin has not yet gone so far in his decision; although he admits that winter can be rather harsh without shelter and provisions and takes advantage of the retreat, it is implied that he is mostly outdoors in warmer seasons. Merlin is a pragmatist.

In keeping with his semi-saintly portrait, Merlin has nothing of the magician about him here. He can be captured and chained. When he refers to Arthur's birth, Merlin mentions nothing about the trick which occasioned the conception. His amazing knowledge is connected with his prophetic powers; he can see ahead to people's deaths, and he can read the stars to know of events present and future. Later, Taliesin mentions Morgen, Avalon's most skilled healer, who can change her shape and can travel in the air:

> Ars quoque nota sibi qua scit mutare figuram
> et resecare novis quasi Dedalus aera pennis.

> Cum vult, est Bristi Carnoti sive Papie,
> cum vult, in vestris ex aere labitur horis. (ll. 922-25)

That Merlin is not given such abilities here, as he is in later works, reinforces that we are presented with a basically historical, understandable world--given that we accept the reality of prophecy and its concomitant powers. The fantastic Morgen is mentioned, but not placed before us, and she is part of a long catalogue of worldwide marvels. Merlin is as much a part of the familiar world as are the kings ruling Britain, not a being from the Other side, or even overtly a demon's son, and his madness is a human madness, resulting from grief.

The second section begins with Taliesin's visit to Merlin in his retreat. Taliesin has been studying with Gildas in Brittany, and Merlin wants to hear what his friend has learned. Perhaps contrary to modern expectation, Merlin does not know everything. Among the items which Taliesin mentions, there is repeated from HRB VI the theory concerning the type of demon (here, "cacodemonibus", clearly uninviting) which was said to be Merlin's father, as confirmed by Maugan from Apuleius:[7]

> et sibi multociens ex aere corpore sumpto
> nobis apparent et plurima sepe sequuntur.
> Quin etiam coitu mulieres agrediuntur
> et faciunt gravidas generantes more prophano. (ll. 781-784)

No comment is made in the VM, by either Merlin or the narrator, on that prior (HRB) explanation of Merlin's birth, and we can bury or recall that connection as we wish. Given Merlin's siblings in the VM, it is hard to allow the story too much credence here, which follows the more Christianized portrait presented to us.

Taliesin's recital goes on for 200 lines (737-940) before Merlin speaks again, reacting to the story of Arthur's committal to Morgen's care. His first words again lament the degeneration of Britain and the renewed Saxon invasions: "Deus nobis ut corrigat insipientes/ has patitur clades ob crimina nostra venire" (ll. 951-52). The return of this theme leads into a recital of the events Merlin has witnessed in his long life, beginning with Vortigern's betrayal of Constans to the recent usurpation of the throne by Conan (ll. 979-1135). Merlin also tells Taliesin the circumstances under which the British will regain the rule of Britain (the similarity of this to what the angel reports to Cadwallader in HRB XII is clear).

Two long catalogues of science and history have interrupted the flow of the narrative. Since what is presented is not new, it is perhaps important to notice the context. Merlin has retreated to the forest to learn about nature; Taliesin aids in that search. What he learns is much the same as what Christian holy men were learning--Taliesin has been with Gildas, a well known Celtic saint.[8] Part of the monk's task in his spiritual growth is to learn what he can of God through the study of His creation. Merlin has begun his spiritual path.

The review of history clarifies the perspective we are supposed to have for the events of this narrative. Merlin claims no role in historical events since the birth of Arthur, mentioning nothing of his role in affairs beyond the prophecies to Vortigern. Taliesin, not Merlin, took Arthur to Morgen. Merlin's later role seems to be that presented at the outset of the VM: respected as a prophet, but also as a prince who leads his men into battle against invading Scots. Merlin is one of the British nobles. The wars the nation has endured since Arthur's departure have touched him personally and prove to be his breaking point. The British have failed to heed the prophet Merlin, and finally the man Merlin turns his back on them, knowing and accepting that God's punishment is on its way.

When the narrative resumes, Merlin's servants have found a new spring at the foot of a mountain which Taliesin and Merlin investigate. When Merlin drinks from the spring, the water fully restores his sanity and equilibrium (for the first time, it seems, since the initial madness after battle). He praises God for his renewed health.

Merlin's chieftains hear that his sanity has been restored and come to ask him again to resume his throne. He refuses, pleading both old age and a preference for the woods.

> Res michi nulla placet que me divellere possit
> ex Calidone mea me judice semper amena.
> Hic ero dum vivam pomis contentis et herbis,
> et mundabo meam pia per jejunia carnem
> ut valeam fungi vita sine fine perhenni. (ll. 1287-91)

Merlin is clearly adopting the hermit's religious life, especially appropriate now that he has regained his sanity, since he can devote himself to this life with his whole mind.

Next, a madman arrives at the spring; Merlin recognizes him and tells his history. This case of madness, from poison, is also cured by the waters of the spring when Merlin suggests it be tried. Invited by Merlin, the man joins the prophet in his retreat, and

Taliesin too decides to be led by Merlin's example and turn away from the world.

The widowed Ganieda joins these three, and the work ends with a new prophetic vision, this time from her lips, a vision of the future--of Geoffrey's twelfth century and the civil wars of Stephen's reign.[9] Merlin accepts this prophecy calmly in the final lines of the narrative:

> Tene, soror, voluit res precantare futuras
> spiritus osque meum compescuit atque libellum?
> Ergo tibi labor iste datur. Leteris in illo
> auspiciisque meis devote singula dicas. (ll. 1521-24)

Having fulfilled his prophetic and historical task, Merlin is free to devote himself entirely to making "a good end" to his life.

This last section reinforces the impressions building earlier and carries through Merlin's retreat to its logical end. Whether one sees this final devotion to God as a conversion from possibly pagan ways or simply as the culmination of a process begun (implied) in the HRB, Merlin's ascetic life is at the end a holy one in the sense any monk's is. To list some of the specific similarities with a saint's life: he is learned; he withdraws from the world; he assists in bringing about a healing miracle and is the subject of one; he is an example to others when a hermit, a leader when in the world; he resists worldly temptation, both of the flesh and of power; and he possesses extraordinary supernatural knowledge and powers of prophecy.

The picture drawn of Merlin adds up in the same way the episodes of a saint's life add up--the holy man is exalted above his peers for reasons demonstrated by God through events on earth. Merlin is true to his prophecies, and if one accepts that his prophecies come from God, the extension is that Merlin is true to God as well--precisely where the British people fail. Geoffrey is, I think, making a case for the elevation of Merlin to "sainthood" because of the prophet's role in events and because of his cumulative example. Geoffrey's reasons for writing the VM can only be speculated upon, but his portrait of Merlin here does, it seems to me, clarify that the British, including Arthur, fail to heed the prophet. While Arthur is presented in a positive way initially, the *speculum regis* reveals his faults as well. Whatever Merlin's faults (or demonic connections) in the HRB, the VM cleanses him.

Although this work had little effect on subsequent Arthurian literature, the elements which did, directly or not, survive (the triple-death prophecy and marketplace prophecies, the wild wooded retreat) place Merlin firmly within the tradition of insular tales. He is later portrayed as learned in the ways of nature, but the classical learning presented in the VM is not in character, nor is the family setting. Merlin's Christian character, however, carries over from the VM, although his actions are mostly derived from the HRB (and the authors' imaginations). Merlin is at essence a loner, and the romances, considered next, build his character with that basic solitariness in mind.

Notes - Chapter Three

[1]L'Histoire de Guillaume le Maréchal, ed. P. Meyer, Société de l'histoire de France, 3 vols., 1891-1901.

[2]See ll. 908-40. All references and quotations are from Basil Clarke's edition of the VM.

[3]For a detailed review of this tradition, see Clarke's introduction to the VM, 22-26, and Appendix One.

[4]Merlin explains that the queen got the leaf in her hair while lying with her lover. Then Ganieda, to convince the king that Merlin is not completely trustworthy, brings a boy before the prophet in three guises. When Merlin foretells three different deaths for the boy, the king's doubts about his wife are allayed. The triple death is fulfilled some years later (ll. 391-415).

[5]Merlin had warned Guendolena, his wife, that if he saw her bridegroom he would kill the new husband. It is interesting that the "vibratum ensem" to which Merlin refers in his warning (l. 380) is in practice "cornua cervo" (l. 467), rather appropriate to his silvestral life; he does kill the man and tries to escape the king's men.

[6]See Clarke 1-5 and notes.

[7]Maugan cites Apuleius' De Deo Socratis as his authority (HRB VI, 18), but Augustine uses this work (acknowledged) in his comments on demons in The City of God, Books 8 and 9, which may be a more likely direct source for Geoffrey.

[8]See Gildas' own writings and the 11th-century Vita Gildae from Britanny.

[9]See Clarke 153, note to ll. 1474-1518, for details of the concordance.

Chapter Four

The King's Right Hand: The Vulgate *Merlin*

The first romance text completely dedicated to Merlin was that of Robert de Boron (late twelfth century), which was intended to serve as the central text of a Grail trilogy. Only 504 lines of the verse text survive,[1] but the prose *Merlin* texts incorporate the story. Alexandre Micha has edited the core of Robert's narrative (in prose), which Micha ends with Arthur's crowning, eliminating the divergent continuations (Robert de Boron, *Merlin*, 293-302). This chapter and the next will deal with two of the continuations, generally known as the Vulgate and Huth *Merlins*, as well as the shared base from Robert. The Vulgate continuation is important because it completes the great cycle of Arthurian texts ranging from *L'Estoire dou Graal* through the *Merlin*, *Lancelot*, *Queste*, to the *Mort Artu*. The Huth text, while surviving incomplete, has been pointed to as Malory's chief source for the relevant books of his work, and it forms part of another cycle J.D. Bruce calls the "Pseudo-Robert" and, more recently, Fanni Bogdanow terms "the post-Vulgate *Roman du Graal*" (11). This cycle is similar to the Vulgate in story line, though it emphasizes different characters and events.[2]

Both prose *Merlins* provide a narrative link between the earlier history of the Grail, its travels with Joseph of Arimathea to Britain, and the chivalric adventures in the prime of Arthur's reign, centering around Lancelot. Also in both, the emphasis is on the founding and development of the Arthurian Court, which separates it from the "original" Grail cycle of Robert, represented most closely today by his Estoire, Micha's edition of Merlin, and the Didot-Perceval.[3] In Robert's cycle, the Court is taken for granted and all adventures are centered around the Grail. While the Vulgate cycle does retain a Grail focus, it is overwhelmed by other matters in the bulk of the cycle (Merlin, Lancelot, and Mort). In the Huth, there is a more personal religious focus, although the preliminaries to the Grail quest still play a major part in the narrative.

All of these texts fit the category of "religious literature" as implied in Hans Robert Jauss' distinction: "In opposition to worldly literature . . . which, by delighting its audience with imaginary topics and heroic deeds, is said to seduce one subtly into idleness and sin, religious poetry insists upon the historical truth of its material, which thus requires of the audience more than mere pleasurable contemplation" ("Levels" 291). Beginning with Robert's story of the Antichrist, as well as the connections to the Joseph story, the texts carry through with a definite insistence on historicity, demonstrated in several ways discussed below.

In Robert, the Vulgate and the Huth, Merlin is the central character. We begin with the story behind Merlin's birth and his youth, then follow him to Vortigern and the sons of Constantine. Through Uter's death and Arthur's ascension, Merlin plays a constant and consistent role in events. Turning to the Vulgate continuation, we follow Merlin, too, away from Britain's history and see him travelling to other lands using his skills, and we watch him fall in love with and lose his freedom to Viviane.

While Merlin's story cannot be told without Britain's, the reverse is also true. He essentially shares top billing with the nation; the narrative alternates between him and the events of Arthur's burgeoning reign, but as other men grow older and experienced enough to perform some of Merlin's self-appointed tasks, he fades from the picture, yielding to the new generation. It is part of his task to set in motion the "proving" of Arthur's knights preliminary to the Grail quest. He makes sure this generation develops properly as part of his active role in affairs, and seems confident that they can continue in the ordained path without his presence and immediate guidance.

Whereas in the later volumes of the Vulgate cycle Merlin is remembered as the prophet of the Grail quest and of the adventures of chivalry--because all that is "seen" of him are inscriptions, prophecies, and set-up adventures which he left behind--in the _Merlin_, he plays a multitude of roles, the primary one mentor to Arthur, much as Gwydion acts for Lleu in _Math_. He is more than a prophet, and his role as magician supports those of mentor and prophet. Although Jean Marx comments that Merlin seems to him to be "plus comme devin que comme prophète" in the Vulgate ("Persistance" 125), I think that the impression comes from the nearly omnipresent supporting role of magic rather than its primary importance to the narrative. In this sense, magic functions much as it does in the _Mabinogi_. The prophet role, in terms of the full cycle, overshadows even his role as Arthur's mentor, and it is a crucial element in setting the historical tone in the work (both Merlin and cycle).[4]

From a very young age, Merlin is possessed of extraordinary knowledge and the equally extraordinary ability to voice it. At the ripe age of 18 months, he comforts his mother to reassure her that she will not be killed because of her illegitimate child. Hearing him, her women proclaim him a devil, and he calls them fools.[5] Given the presence of this motif in saints' lives, it is not a sufficient indicator of his nature. Physically, Merlin advances quickly, since at nine months he is as big as a two-year-old.

When the judge comes to try Merlin's mother for her supposed crime, the child Merlin not only proves her innocence, but reveals that the judge's mother committed adultery with her priest, the judge's true father. Merlin explains how his powers came to him:

> Ie uoel que tu saces & croies que ie sui fils a .i. anemi qui engigna ma mere. & saces que tel maniere danemi ont a non esquibedes & repairent en lair. & diex a souffert que iaie lor sens & lor memoire si sai les coses qui sont faites & dites & alees & par ce sai iou loeure ta mere. Et nostre sires qui souffri & uaut que ie eusse ce en memoire par la bonte ma mere & por sa sainte uraie repentance & por la penitance que cis preudoms qui chi est li encharga & por le commandement de sainte eglize quele crut ma diex doune tant de uertu que ie sai les choses que a uenir sont & ce poes vous aperceuoir par ce que ie vous dirai. (17)

Immediately Merlin issues his first prediction, that the guilty priest will drown himself; the prediction comes true (18).

When confronted with this amazing child, the holy man Blaise puts him to a test of faith to be sure he is not still demonic (18-19). Again we hear how God preserved and enhanced Merlin's powers.

This repetition--three times in six pages--of Merlin's redemption by God brings home, first, the child's extraordinary nature, and second, God's ability to turn evil plans to His own ends. The narrative begins with devils plotting to regain their hold over men, broken by Christ, by having one of their own father Christ's alter-ego, i.e., the Antichrist. Merlin was planned to be mankind's downfall, and the rechanneling of his fate can be accomplished only by God. Because Merlin's mother was an unwilling victim who turned to her confessor immediately, God was able to use the child Himself. All that is left to Merlin of his father are his hairy body ("plus velu & plus de poil", 12) and the demonic powers, which he will now use to positive ends. Far from being man's downfall, Merlin's redemption re-emphasizes the powerful redemption of man through Christ. Later, in the course of revealing to Uter the history behind the Round Table, Merlin once again tells how he was allowed his demonic powers by God as he reassures Uter of the correct path to follow. Here Merlin explains that knowledge of the past is from his demonic heritage, but knowledge of the future comes from God, and that with God's gift he himself knows how not to do the devils' will.

The fact that the narrator as well as Merlin informs us of God's intentions, and that the good Blaise remains convinced of Merlin's goodness, forces the reader to accept that Merlin is indeed no devil and his actions are not evil. It is, of course, crucial to the narrative that Merlin's acts not be questioned, and Robert ensures this attitude from the start.

The use of the religious marvellous immediately puts us on a very different level from most early romances. Not only is the marvellous given a clear source, God (unlike in Chrétien, for example), but it also takes the narrative from the "timeless" Celtic realm into the real world where events can be dated by reference to Christ's birth. Since this work follows the Joseph of Arimathea text, the historical connection is doubly clear. In fact, the religious nature of the marvellous lends a hagiographical atmosphere to the work, placing the initial motivation for events with God rather than man.[6] Lagorio similarly describes the Joseph volume: "[it] exhibits all the characteristics of an hagiographical romance and might well be subtitled, 'The Apocryphal Acts of Joseph of Arimathea and his Grail apostolate'" ("Joseph" 56).

Interestingly, Merlin tells Blaise that if the devils had chosen his grandmother, whose evil ways set the events in motion, to bear him, they would have succeeded in their plan. That they did not indicates, first, that the mother of Antichrist (to parody Christ) must be a virgin; second, that the devils delight in destruction, since they destroy the entire family, one by one, before getting to Merlin's mother. Their nature dooms the Antichrist plan from the start.

When Vortigern's clerks advise killing Merlin, they do so because they "saw" him as the cause of their own deaths. The contrast between "bad magic" (pagan) and Merlin's "good magic" is demonstrated by Merlin's reaction. While he does completely discredit them and reads them a lecture on dabbling in necromancy, he speaks for their lives when they promise to quit this practice. The clerks, clearly, did not foresee correctly; I can imagine the demons once again trying to regain Merlin, or at least eliminate this misadventure.[7] Since the clerks drew upon non-Christian means of divination, the demons could have misled them to that end. In any case, the redeemed Merlin, now about eight years old, demonstrates here that he does indeed know how to use his powers well and does not use them for revenge upon the clerks.

After the episode with Vortigern, Merlin pays the first of many visits to Blaise, now in Northumberland. The purpose of these visits is threefold. First, for the narrator, Merlin cannot always be at the hub of events and this gives him a useful retreat. Second, Merlin explains that his demonic heritage has given him the urge to be alone (43). Finally, the visits are to provide Blaise with material for the book Merlin "commissioned" from him to follow on the Grail history. Just as Geoffrey traced Britain's origins to Troy, Robert and his successors are interested in connecting Britain to the Holy Land and Holy Family, hence to human salvation and church history.

The recurring line à propos the visits is, "et Blaise le mist tout en son liure par le quel nous le sauons encore" (35). In other words, we are basically reading Blaise's book, which he wrote straight from Merlin's reports. What greater authority could one ask for? Merlin serves not only his contemporaries with the gift of his supernatural knowledge, but he also leaves the legacy of his knowledge to "us" via Blaise's book. This is, of course, a contrivance of the author to provide his work the veracity a history[8] should have, but what an appropriate conceit: to symbolize the omniscient narrator with Merlin's supernatural, God-given omniscience.

When Pandragon and Uter enter the scene, Merlin's prophetic presence is enhanced by his abilities in shape-changing and engineering, in addition to the battle strategy which I will discuss later. Merlin's first encounters with the brothers are in disguise. The purpose behind these various disguises is obscure. With Pandragon, it could be to test the king's reactions to the poor men of Merlin's disguises, or to reveal to the king one way which Merlin might be useful to him. With Uter, Merlin's old-man disguise helps to give credence to the warning he bears, and the alternation later between the boy and the old man is expressly "por aus metre en ioie & en bele risee" (41). While this love of trickery may be left over from the demonic in him, Merlin's playful attitude is in stark contrast to the destructive trickery we see aimed at his mother's family. Although Merlin asks the king and Uter to keep his shape-changing secret (even they, however, do not ever see the transformations take place), others will learn of it as time goes on.

Merlin uses his power of disguise again when Uter battles for Igerne. First, when Ulfin looks for him, Merlin appears as an old man and a cripple, but Uter recognizes Merlin's behavior and Merlin comes to the king's tent then in his usual appearance. Then, after exacting a promise from Uter to grant an unspecified request, Merlin changes himself, Ulfin, and Uter with "vne herbe" so they look like the duke and two of his men for the famous night assault on Tintagel when Arthur is conceived. These latter disguises wash off with water.

The illustrations in the British Library Add. Ms. 10292 of the Vulgate and the Huth ms. point up contemporary understanding of Merlin's appearance. Although none of them picture him (old or young) with a hairy body, he clearly first appears as a child, to Vortigern and Ambrosius (and even at Uter's deathbed), and his shape-changing is a total transformation in size, costume, and face. In his "normal" appearance as an adult, he is not distinguished by any unusual mark in the miniatures.

There are some barons, of course, who doubt Merlin's abilities and one of them devises a test to prove that Merlin is not so knowledgeable as he seems. In almost a parody of Merlin's own powers, the baron comes forward in three different appearances and asks Merlin what his death will be. Each time, Merlin gives a different answer, but he assures the king afterward that the triple-death will come to pass. Pandragon believes Merlin and will not dismiss him as advisor, the baron's aim, unless the baron's death disproves Merlin's prophecy.

The triple-death motif is an echo of Geoffrey's _Vita_, in both cases being used supposedly to discredit Merlin but actually proving him right. Here, the contrast between the baron's attempt to discredit through disguise and false prophecy, and Merlin's own real powers of disguise and prophecy illustrates the rightness of

Merlin's position beside the king. As a result of this trickery, however, Merlin vows never to speak clear prophecies again in public; only after the fact will his words be completely understood, he says. The king, therefore, orders a record be kept of Merlin's words so they can be remembered at the proper time. This explains the change we see in his utterances, as well as "explains" the contemporary existence of independent books of his prophecies (cf. those edited by Lucy Paton).

Immediately after this development, Merlin privately tells the brothers of a returning Saxon invasion. They ask if either will die in the battle, and Merlin, after some stalling, finally says that one of them will. He vows to create a famous "cymentiere" on the battle site (Salisbury). It is interesting that here Stonehenge is erected as Pandragon's memorial; in Geoffrey, the elder brother orders the circle built as a memorial to the Britons slain treacherously by Saxons, though he is eventually interred there himself. In the Vulgate, the circle is purely Merlin's tribute to the king, who is slain in battle (not poisoned--Merlin's "protection" would seem non-existent were that carried over from Geoffrey) defending his realm. Merlin moves the stones "par force dart" (53), but aside from the expected amazement on the part of Uter (now Uterpandragon) and others, the episode is passed by quickly in favor of what follows--Uter's founding of the Round Table.

Merlin suggests the table to Uter as an honorable and holy deed, setting the scene for the Last Supper-Grail, Joseph-Grail,

Arthur-Grail trinity of tables. With Uter's consent, Merlin has the table built, and at Pentecost this third table is seated with fifty knights chosen by Merlin. All these events clearly identify the future of the Table, the knights, and eventually the Grail quest with Merlin. Merlin chooses the original knights, whom we will encounter again when Arthur marries and gains possession of the table from Leodegan (how Leodegan gets the table is never mentioned). The "empty seat," too, is Merlin's doing, the seat which awaits Galahad in a later volume. The baron who prematurely tests the seat disappears, and Merlin, returning after two years' absence, lectures the remaining knights on how the table and seat should be honored, not lightly tested, for the one who will safely occupy the seat and complete the circle which Judas broke has yet to be born (57-58).

After Uter's liaison with Igerne and the duke's death, negotiations are put in motion to marry Igerne to the king. Throughout the preliminary episodes, Igerne has behaved very loyally to her husband and is pictured as a chaste, honorable woman. She truly believes it is the duke who comes to her at Tintagel, and a parallel with Merlin's mother underlies the events; both women are Christian, taken unknowing. Igerne later tells Uter honestly what happened that night at Tintagel, that a man "en la semblance de son seignor" came to her. She seems unsure now that it was the duke, and she does not hide her doubt from Uter (who of course knows the truth, and does not tell her). Since Merlin's mother's holy life played a large part in Merlin's redemption (as well as her own), the emphasis on Igerne's innocence reflects positively in its turn on Arthur. Although Uter is no demon, the adultery is un-Christian. Merlin comments that the sin of deceiving her weighs on him, but implies that his fostering of the child away from court will help him atone (74). In light of the good effect this adultery will have on the country, the sin, all things considered, is venial.[9] There is no clear conclusion drawn concerning Arthur's actual legitimacy, except the favor shown him by divine intervention at his election and indirectly throughout his relationship with Merlin.[10]

All of Merlin's deeds have up to now laid the groundwork for Arthur and his reign. The Round Table with its knights and empty seat, the deception of Igerne, and the fostering of Arthur in secrecy all set the stage for later events. Merlin's place beside Pandragon and Uter also sets a precedent for him to assume a similar place by Uter's son (just as Ulfin does), with the authority of experience behind him.

The barons turn to Merlin after Uter's death, first, because he is at Uter's deathbed and actually provokes the king to speech after he had been "dead" three days. At this time, only Merlin was near enough to hear Uter's actual words. Second, they defer to Merlin because of his wisdom and great love for the king, and they trust him to guide their choice responsibly (79). This avowal now of trust in Merlin points up their later irresponsible rebellion when a sixteen-year-old boy is set on the throne. Merlin supports the boy, and more important, the direct support of God is indicated by means of the famous sword-in-stone episode, which in turn convinces the priests, bishops, and archbishops to rally behind him. By this point, it is fruitless to ask whether Merlin set up the sword or not, since if he did, we know he acted on God's behalf. Merlin does visit Blaise during the critical period of the sword's appearance at Christmas, the re-testing of Arthur's right to it at Easter, and the coronation at Pentecost, putting the new king in the spotlight and forestalling any talk that Merlin might be tricking the barons. With the support of the clerical community and the commoners, Arthur is placed on the throne, but the highest barons remain unhappy, in spite of Arthur's innate charm and generosity.

The manuscripts diverge at this point. Micha's choice of endings for Robert's "original" story comes from the Didot and Modena manuscripts, in which Merlin comes to court and reveals Arthur's parentage, whereupon the barons accept him--once they know he is highborn. Arthur honors Merlin, and the story proceeds to the Perceval-Quest.

The Vulgate mss. take the story in a different direction entirely. After his coronation, Arthur calls his barons to court, honors them, and provides them with rich gifts, which they refuse to accept, defying him. At this juncture, Merlin reappears. Although he and Ulfin present their testimony and evidence regarding Arthur's birth, some barons still refuse to accept him, laying siege to the town. When Merlin advises them from the walls to give up their rebellion, they laugh at him.

In this part, the term "li enchanteres" is used by the narrator for the first time in referring to Merlin. It may well be, among other evidence, merely an indication of a new author (not Robert de Boron) coming into the picture, but it also gives an indication of Merlin's enlarging role in which he more and more uses his magical powers to direct the affairs of Britain.

The remainder of the Vulgate _Merlin_ is taken up primarily with the rebellion of the barons and other wars, but I will consider the martial aspect of Merlin's role below. Several episodes which show Merlin in non-martial situations break up the war scenes, and since the events of the narrative take place over a period of about three and a half years, the breaks are realistic as well as desirable.[11]

In his visits to Blaise, Merlin reveals many future events, sometimes in clear, but usually in obscure, language; generally, the near future is clearer than the distant. Paramount is Merlin's knowledge of his own fate, along with that of Britain and her allies. During one visit, Merlin tells Blaise of dire future events, then comments:

> mais iou feroie pecie se iou destournoie ce que nostre sires ma doune tant de sens & de discretion come iai por aidier acomplir les auentures del saint graal qui doiuent estre acomplies & traites a fin au tans le roy artu. Mais ne vous chaut de moi plus enquerre car bien saures encore que ce porra estre. & vous meismes le uerres a vos iex ains que vous morres ce sacies de voir. (207)

Merlin later takes the same resigned, obedient attitude with regard to his own fate, imprisonment by Viviane.

The affair with Viviane shows Merlin at his weakest; it is as if he must fall in love all the harder as an exchange for his supernatural gifts. He "falls" in a purely human manner and appears weaker than other men, perhaps because of its contrast with his otherwise dominant role. Merlin gradually teaches Viviane all she wants to know--all she can know without being half-demon like Merlin. She at first seems taken up by the excitement of learning from him, granting him love only in exchange for information, but as the narrative returns to them again and again, she seems genuinely fond of him as well. She does not abandon him in his prison, although she alone can visit him there (452, 461).

This affair is fated, and Merlin is not ignorant of his fate. Viviane's grandmother, the goddess Diane, gave her son a gift, that his first daughter "soit tant couoitie del plus sage homme terrien apres ma mort que au tans vertiger de la bloie bertaigne commenchere a regner & quil li enseng la grignor partie de son sens" (209). Merlin, from his conversations with Blaise, clearly knows what he is getting into from the beginning and does nothing to avert it, even though he recognizes its foolishness and its consequences (209). The enchanter's fate, like that of Britain later, is tied up with human love, the society and its "creator" both victims of earthly weaknesses.

In narrative terms, the affair with Viviane allows Merlin to disappear as he must; this volume of the cycle was written last (Micha, "The Vulgate Merlin," ALMA, 323), so its author likely conformed to the design already in place (as reflected in other episodes, too). But in one major way Merlin's behavior has been changed. At the beginning of the Lancelot, Merlin and Viviane's affair is also presented, but there Merlin is much more the son of the lusty devil who begat him; he repeatedly tries to get Viviane to lie with him, and the arcane knowledge she learns from him saves her virginity. She imprisons him to be freed from his advances.[12] The _Merlin_ text only suggests the sexual overtures, and Viviane shows no signs of fear, making for a consistent role for the prophet in the volume. In the _Lancelot_, Viviane must appear in a more positive light because of her fostering of Lancelot--as Merlin in the earlier text must because of his relationship with Arthur.

The knowledge Viviane gains from Merlin is put to important use when she saves and rears Lancelot[13] as well as when she intervenes in later episodes in the cycle, as if keeping events on track on Merlin's behalf. Before he is imprisoned by Viviane, Merlin also teaches Arthur's sister Morgain. This, too, will have an important bearing on future events; Morgain's use of her powers for evil contrasts with Viviane's goodness. This difference, too, stresses the Lady of the Lake's (Viviane's) inheritance of Merlin's position as enchanter, while at the same time demonstrating how both Merlin and Viviane resist the temptations of their powers to do harm. Morgain does not have their strength of character.

In another break between battles, Merlin arranges a one-night affair between King Ban and Agravadain's daughter, using magic to assure the safe consummation which will result in Lancelot's half-brother Hector (404-405, 446). So again Merlin arranges an illicit, adulterous liaison for the sake of the future; Arthur, too, met with Lisanor early in the romance with Merlin's help, engendering Lohot (124).[14] That affair was not adulterous, but it was without the sanction of marriage. These various liaisons, like Uter's, are not openly condemned by the narrator, who accepts them as part of the normal conduct of life, or at least necessary to the conduct of the cycle. Arthur's incest, alone of the affairs, is condemned, and even that liaison is passed over quickly and given no great emphasis.[15] Arthur "copies" his father's trick, in that the sister believes her husband has lain with her until Arthur reveals the truth. Neither realized at that time their affair was incestuous. It is, I think, important that Merlin has no part in the conception of Mordred (aiding or hindering), leaving the responsibility on Arthur himself.

Merlin travels to the far ends of Europe in two escapades; in one he simply directs a Saracen king into Christianity by interpreting a dream.[16] Merlin's words to the king issue from an invisible body, which of course strengthens the force of his message. Some of this king's grandsons come to Arthur's court later. The Grisandole episode in Rome is much longer, and Merlin's miscellaneous magical talents are again on display. He appears in the shape of a stag, as a wild man, a dream interpreter, the knowing "laugher" again, and as prophet. He reveals his true identity after he leaves, through writing on a wall, and he returns to Blaise from Rome in 24 hours "de fort art" (281-92). The Grisandole sequence shows several affinities to the _Vita Merlini_--the adulterous queen; the three laughs; the connection between Merlin, the wild man, and the stag; and the various prophetic utterances--but all is adapted to fit the new story well. The only overt connection from this episode to the story line in the cycle, though, is his prophecy of fighting between Rome and Britain which occurs at the end of this volume.

The Grisandole story provides a break between two important episodes of war, at Benoic where Arthur and company are successful, then at Clarence where the rebels lose to the Saxons. Merlin keeps busy, in full control of his powers (even though he is teaching Viviane already). One could argue, I think, that Merlin maintains his role of controlling future events with this episode: since Britain will fight Rome, Roman history must be made to coincide properly, hence Merlin's interference in Rome's affairs. The same would hold true of his role with the Saracen king regarding the grandsons who come to Arthur.

Although the magic-prophetic aspect of Merlin's role is the first one we see, it shares equal importance with his position as counsellor-strategist in the conduct of Arthur's wars (and, to some extent, Pandragon and Uter's) and in the progress of Arthur's political and personal life. Merlin's first involvements in war are indirect; he warns Uter of a surprise attack, tells the brothers of upcoming invasions, advises them beforehand on the best array and plan of attack, and assures Uter a final victory. In none of the martial encounters involving Pandragon and Uter does Merlin appear during or in battle. They are seasoned warriors and can conduct their own wars. With Arthur, however, Merlin is from the first at his side, actually deciding on strategy, directing forces, and carrying the king's banner on the field.[17] Arthur, we remember, is sixteen, newly knighted at his coronation,[18] and without any concerted education in kingship. He needs Merlin's help.

We have seen this counsellor-king relationship in the work before, when Vortigern stood beside Constans. Unlike the ambitious Vortigern, Merlin has no desire to usurp the kingship for himself, and his efforts are directed at making Arthur self-sufficient as ruler, whereas Vortigern aimed at keeping Constans dependent. This pairing of opposites again emphasizes Merlin's positive role.

For the nonce, Kay is but a figurehead seneschal--he carries Arthur's banner when Merlin gives it to him--while Merlin performs the active duties of seneschal, and more. Merlin as ambassador for Arthur arranges for Ban and Bors to come from Brittany to help the young king, promising the brothers that their lands will be safe in their absence. They bring with them Guinebaus, a wise cleric,[19] who questions Merlin and determines he is acceptable (106). Once again, Merlin is pronounced "clean."

After several engagements, the rebels are scattered, and to add to their loss, they discover that Saxons have invaded their lands back home while they fought Arthur. At Merlin's suggestion, Arthur leaves a token force behind and moves the army to help Leodegan at Carmelide. Here Merlin takes full charge. He carries the banner, opens the gate by his magic at the best time to attack, creates a storm among the enemy so they can barely see, and gallops all over the field directing one man to rescue another. The giant Rions is personally defeated by Arthur, who confronts him at Merlin's insistence. Merlin's "sens" and "force" are given equal credit with the fighting men for the victory (156). This first victory against the Saxons takes place on Ascension Day, emphasizing its holy-war atmosphere.

In Arthur's first two battles, against rebels and against Saxons, he is successful. Clearly Merlin is the driving force, the brain, behind these battles. The barons recognize his importance, too: "et sacies," says Brangoires, "que tant comme merlins sera encontre nous naurons nous ia au roy artu duree" (125). In battle Merlin is never without his magic; aside from the knowledge of who is in trouble, he creates storms, sets fires, induces fog, and forms streams to disconcert the enemy. One of his most effective pieces of magic against the Saxons involves carrying the dragon banner with fire shooting from the dragon's mouth. (This fire also sheds light during night maneuvers.) The Saxons flee, and the same tactic later succeeds against Ban and Bors' enemies in Britanny.

Merlin repeats his magical help several times as Arthur fights, but he never uses his magic to harm others directly, nor does he take up weapons. Arthur notices this and comments to Bors,

> que moult a preudomme en merlin & sans faille il estoit plains de proece & fors de cors & de menbres. . . . Mais nous ne trouons pas lisant quil mesist onques main sor homme por lui mal faire mais souent auenoit que quant il estoit en presse de gent quil abatoit del pis del cheval & homme & cheval. (272)

Viviane, too, never tries to harm, and it seems that the temptation to use harmful magic, even on the side of "good", is one to be resisted.

At one point, Merlin begins a charge by calling on the Blessed Virgin Mary (220), and generally encourages a quasi-crusader ethic in fighting the Saxons. In the climactic battle, Arthur's side carries a banner bearing a red cross, reminiscent of the crusades, and in the battle for Carmelide, Sadoynes admonishes the Christians:

> si defendons nos uies & nos hiretages encontre les anemis ihesu crist. & cil qui moura por sainte cretiente defendre sauf sera & garis ne iamais naurons si grant mestier donor recheuoir comme nous auons ore. (226-27)

This echoes strongly of Turpin's address in the _Chanson de Roland_, and elsewhere in the _Merlin_ we see a repetition of this shared attitude, "Paien ont tort e chrestien ont dreit" (_Roland_, l. 1015).

Aside from helping Arthur in battle, Merlin helps him indirectly by interfering in the anti-Saxon battles being fought by Gawain and the other young nephews of the king back at Camelot. The rebels, too, fight on against the Saxons. They are without their sons, who have rallied to Arthur's side, with their mothers' encouragement, and the rebels' heavy losses against the Saxons compared with their sons' victories clearly show who is on the "right" side. In this part, the scene moves back and forth between the rebels on the one hand and Arthur or his nephews on the other, emphasizing by contrast the wrong and the right. This picture of the noble rebels leans heavily toward satire, showing them floundering against the pagan hordes, beating hasty retreats, and encountering a variety of problems. They are fighting against God's will as well as against a physical enemy, and the first causes failure in the second.

In one episode, Lot orders his wife to take the youngest son (Mordred, a babe in arms) and flee to another castle, and she runs right into Saxon hands. Merlin, disguised as a knight, alerts Gawain to the troop of Saxons nearby, and Gawain manages to defeat them and rescue his mother, again emphasizing which side (Gawain's, not Lot's) is in the right. Merlin's many disguises and ability to travel quickly allow him to direct the young men to the most advantageous ambushes, alert them to others in trouble, and generally manage affairs to the king's advantage.

In the course of these many battles, the secret of Merlin's shape-changing gradually becomes more widely known. Arthur first learns of it through an episode in which Merlin appears as a low-born duck hunter;[21] Ulfin and Bretel inform the king of the magic at work (122). Merlin plays similar tricks on Arthur intermittently. Gawain learns of Merlin's abilities from Dos (205) after being led from place to place by mysterious, disappearing knights, boys, and old men. Far from being angered by the trickery, Gawain recognizes the help he has been given and is anxious to meet Merlin, as Merlin. When he does, the young knight offers his service and develops a great love for Merlin (257) which Merlin returns because he sees Gawain's loyalty to Arthur. When asked, Gawain promises to keep silent about Merlin's abilities to avoid drawing envious attention to Merlin.

Entwined among and between the battles, Merlin devotes a large amount of time to educating Arthur in the attitudes of a king and arranges an important step in the affairs of state--choosing a queen. It is Merlin whom Leodegan approaches concerning the possibility of a marriage (159, 216), and Arthur here plays less the role of king than of prince, with a "father" arranging his marriage.

While never usurping the role of a priest, Merlin does remind Arthur occasionally that God is the source of his good fortune; he had previously spoken to Pandragon and Uter of the duties of a king, mentioning there, too, that God came first. To Arthur, he says, "Sire, ore esgardes que nostre a fuit por vous & por vostre peuple saluer & garantir. moult en deues dieu loer & gracier de boin cuer" (385). He expressed similar sentiments when addressing Uter about the Round Table, concentrating on the ethical and spiritual ideals crucial to salvation. Merlin wants these ideals established in Britain to prepare the way for the Quest.

Merlin also advises Arthur on such matters as preparing a proper reception for visitors, distributing largesse (although Arthur did well instinctively in that area even before his coronation), sending emissaries, and proper battlefield behavior. During the battle to free Ban and Bors' lands from usurpers, Merlin scolds Arthur and his men for "cowardice" and Arthur feels "moult grant paor que merlins ne fust courecies a lui" (271). While such negative inducement to heroics is not unusual, Merlin obviously has taken on an authoritative role in Arthur's life. This authority, however, does not exclude him from Arthur's close friendship. When Leodegan wants to hurry his daughter's wedding, Arthur says he must wait:

> Mais il me faut le millor ami ke iou ai. ne sans li nespouserai ie mie. Et quant li rois leodegans oi ce si le demanda qui cis amis estoit. & il dist que ce estoit merlins car par lui auoit recoure tout le bien & lonor kil auoit. (299)

Later, Arthur offers to reward Merlin with whatever he wants (378); Merlin effectively avoids the offer by changing the topic, warning the king that there is trouble brewing among his knights.

After Arthur's wedding, tournaments are held in celebration and serious fighting breaks out between the Round Table knights and Gawain's contingent. Despite several admonitions, the trouble continues. The initial free-for-all is stopped, but further ambushes and insults exacerbate the situation. Merlin points out that jealousy is the root cause, and making Gawain a member of the Round Table works to curb the enmity. Meanwhile, all jousting and tournaments are banned at Guenevere's insistence.[22] She shows herself an able queen, capable of inspiring fierce loyalty and also of dealing with its consequences.

The various scenes of Guenevere and Arthur together, from their earliest shy kisses and glances through their holding court in peace, provide an important picture of a couple fit not only for each other but also for their positions. These scenes firmly establish the affection, loyalty and devotion that Arthur and Guenevere build up for each other, a picture which must be recalled when problems arise in later volumes. From the prophecies Merlin utters, it is obvious that he knows Guenevere will cause trouble for Arthur, but he fulfills his task of bringing the two together (thereby also returning the Round Table to Uter's son). Merlin's political actions are rooted in his religious mission, and the furtherance of the religious ends always takes precedence.

Before the climactic battle with the Saxons, Arthur and the rebels are reconciled. The united troops are victorious. Although Merlin plays a large part in the battle, Gawain--now Arthur's constable and heir--has successfully played the role of ambassador as well as knight. His character and adventures are a major focus of the second half of the work, making it the "enfances" of Gawain along with Arthur. Until Lancelot's arrival (in the next volume), Gawain is Arthur's Best Knight. His later friendship for Lancelot speaks well for him in that he holds no grudge over losing his pre-eminence.[23] This younger generation is ready to take on the role Merlin has thus far played, but Merlin hangs on for the victory against Rome, plus Arthur's defeats of the Giant of Mont St. Michel and the Cat of Lausanne, before he takes his final leave.

When Merlin does go, Arthur and Guenevere are worried and upset. The king, thinking Merlin will return like before, says,

> moult doucement. biaus amis merlin vous en ires. ne iou ueul vous puis retenir sour uostre pois. mais moult serai a malaise iusques a tant que ie uous reuoie pour dieu hastes vous dont del reuenir. Sire fait merlins chest le daerraine fois. & a dieu vous commant. Quant li rois loy quil dist chest la daerraine fois. si en fu moult esbahis. et merlins sen parti sans plus dire tout en plourant. (450-51)

Arthur waits seven weeks, then sends Gawain and thirty others to seek Merlin. Significantly, Gawain has the honor of finding the magician. Invisible, Merlin speaks to him from the hidden prison in Broceliande and explains what has happened. After Gawain leaves, he says, only Viviane will be able to speak with him. When Gawain expresses surprise at the wise Merlin's fate, the prisoner tells him, "iou fui si fols que iaim plus autrui que moi" (461). Merlin loses, essentially, his spiritual freedom and his ability to act for God by giving in to human weakness. He sends Gawain on his way, commending "le roi artus & le royalme de logres & vous & tous lez barons" to the care of God. Grieving, Gawain returns to Wales. Merlin's final farewell to Gawain also helps the young knight, who had been transformed into a dwarf in a misadventure staged, it is implied, by Viviane, recover his true shape. Thus, the volume ends with the first "romance" quest and adventure and that honor, too, belongs to Gawain.

Merlin's final scenes with Arthur, Blaise, Viviane, and Gawain show him at his most human, appropriate for his "fall" from supernaturalistic authority in the realm. Like the Grail, Merlin has a kind of mystery about him, a deliberately maintained veil of obscurity. Some elements of his powers he keeps hidden, just as his prophecies are obscure after the baron's attempted deception. The characters closest to him (with the possible exception of Blaise) are left unaware of it, but he has arranged in one way or another all the crucial, and some trivial, events in Britain's future.

Arthur's legitimacy and right to the throne are now unquestioned, the country's Christianity and freedom from external enemies assured. Miscellaneous future adventures have been arranged for the knights and, above all, news of the Grail has surfaced in Britain (334-35) and the necessary elements are present and waiting to be put in motion for the quest. Merlin's prophecies lead to the Grail quest and beyond; when Arthur's army meets the Saxons in the climactic battle of the *Merlin*, Merlin sadly refers to a day when Salisbury Plain will again see such a large battle array: "que li fils ochira le pere & lie peres le fil & ce sera en ceste misme place & a celui jour demoura la terre de la grante bertaigne sans signors & sans hoir" (385).

The combination of generic elements in this one work, even more than in the cycle as a whole, make it difficult to classify according to traditional norms. We have seen *chanson de geste*/epic elements in the rebellions and battles, saint's life elements in the story of Merlin, romance elements in Arthur's court and Gawain's adventures, and, overshadowing all of these, historical elements in the unrolling of Britain's fated path. While the "history" is actually pseudo-history, it is treated as true; Bloch commented that the cycle "is, at bottom, the literary form of pseudo-history" (207).

We know where this episode in Britain's story stands in relation to the life of Christ, the commonest measure of time in the Middle Ages. The biographical stories (Merlin's, Arthur's, Gawain's, and later Lancelot's) add another historical dimension, though this motif alone would not be enough since it is found in a number of medieval narratives. Within the *Merlin*, reference is made to previous earthly events (i.e., in the Joseph story), to divine events (the plot of the devils to counter Christ's influence), and to future events both earthly and divine (the future of the characters and of the Grail). The motif of prophecy itself presumes an historical outlook. While we may not see this Arthur as an historical figure, the author treats him as such; at the very least, the "real Arthur" has been appropriated into a vast legend, that legend being treated as history. Rather than the truncated vision of courtly life presented in the earlier verse romances, the Vulgate Merlin shows us a more realistic picture, one in which barons rebel, Saxons invade, and tournaments degenerate into riots.

Later in the cycle, the Mort reverses the Merlin's epic/romance balance; where the latter begins with epic and ends with romance, the former tragically turns around the sequence. The question of fate looms large, and God's direction is difficult to see after the Quest ends unless we keep in mind Merlin's prophecies and his God-given role in directing the future. Merlin is very sure of every step he takes, and this assurance does not easily admit alternative paths. Although he does on occasion perform what seems gratuitous magic, God's gift obviously allows him the leeway to create amusement as well as awe, earning him a place within society, not on its borders. In the cycle both magic and the mysterious, though functioning as in the Celtic tales, are finally tied to God.

The Vulgate Merlin is very concerned with the establishment of a stable social order. This society will be host to divine events and the stage must be properly set. However, the same forces which lead to an intense spiritual experience also lead to a dramatic social disintegration. The necessity of a strict adherence to Christian teachings is clear. A stable society requires it.

Merlin's redemption through baptism and his subsequent ability to work for the good of Britain are undermined by human weaknesses, his own and others'. These weaknesses emphasize the need for mankind's redemption through Christ as well as the need for the social group to be directed along Christian paths. Because the men who lead this society stray, the social experiment ultimately fails. Although the Merlin maintains its own narrative integrity, it also prepares us for future developments in the kingdom.

Merlin's character in the Vulgate, then, reflects both the strengths and finally the weaknesses of the society he helps found. His story is a microcosm of the Vulgate saga, his magic a mirror of the pervasive presence of God. While individuals, of course, make up society, the larger community is more important here; the fate of Merlin mirrors the fate of the Arthurian society which mirrors the fate of humanity as a whole.

The tragedy is a universal one, reversible only through a thoroughly Christian life, for which read a monastic life. The Vulgate cycle is a product of the Cistercian movement (Frappier, ALMA, 306-7, 317) and reflects its ethos to a greater or lesser degree throughout. The devotion required of members of society to achieve a non-tragic finale can, it seems, only be accomplished in the cloister.[24] The temptations, especially the descendants of Eve, to which the Arthurians fall prey are worldly. The monastic direction at the end of the Mort points the way. Arthur, falling in battle, does not have Lancelot's chance to redeem his sins. Lancelot, however, turns to the religious life and is suitably rewarded at his death: "[les angles] enportoient lasus el ciel l'ame de nostre frere Lancelot" (*Mort* 261).

In the post-Vulgate *Roman du Graal*, the monastic ethos disappears. The emphasis is still religious, but a more personal, worldly, approach to religion replaces the communal. In the Huth continuation, Merlin's character and role within the narrative also change to suit this shift.

Notes - Chapter Four

[1]Robert's fragment is printed in: Robert de Boron, Le Roman de L'Estoire dou Graal, ed. William A. Nitze, 126-30; and Robert de Boron, Merlin: Roman du XIIIe siècle, ed. Alexandre Micha, 1-17.

[2]See Bruce, 463-70, and Bogdanow, The Romance of the Grail for details about the post-Vulgate cycle, which has been "reconstructed" from independent pieces; this cycle, unlike the Vulgate, is not found integrated into one set of manuscripts.

[3]See Nitze and Micha, supra, and William Roach, ed., The Didot Perceval according to the Manuscripts of Modena and Paris. In the Didot Perceval, Merlin's end comes after Arthur's (as in the Vita Merlini), and it is a voluntary retreat, not an imprisonment.

[4]Paul Zumthor sees the same tendency, that the motif of prophecy provides an historical perspective to the whole ("Merlin" 156).

[5]Lestoire de Merlin, 13-14. All subsequent references in the text of this chapter are to this edition.

[6]Morton W. Bloomfield comments on the saint's life's motivation being centered above, rather than in, this world (118). He also notes, regarding time in epic and romance, that the epic "has a historical or pseudo-historical dimension," that epic episodes are "rational," with motivation found in the story; romance has a "timelessness" which is "frequently created by placing it in the far-distant past" (105, 116). All of these elements can be applied to the Merlin, indeed to the complete cycle, which complicates the question of generic classification for the work(s), as I have noted.

[7]In Merlin le Prophète, Paul Zumthor also sees the possibility of demonic interest in the astrologers' attempt to have Merlin killed (147).

[8]There is some disagreement as to whether the word estoire is specific, i.e., used for a claim to veracity, or is interchangeable with roman in the 12th and 13th centuries. Richard Hartman holds the former view (35), and Paul Zumthor in his Essai (348) expresses the latter. The Grand Larousse gives no direct differentiation, but notes under the entry for histoire that its use around the twelfth century refers to "relation d'événements, de faits réels et généralement remarkables à quelque titre, particuliers à un ou à plusieurs individus." By 1462, however, the meaning has expanded to include a recital of events all or in part imaginary. Under roman, the use (ca. 1140-1400) refers to merely "oeuvre narrative d'une certaine longeur, écrite en langue romane, d'abord en vers, puis en prose, et d'inspiration variée." Here, too, specific reference to

fictional content is postponed, in this case to the sixteenth century. At the time of the Vulgate's appearance, then, it seems that _estoire_ implied veracity.

[9]See Alexandre Micha, _Étude sur le "Merlin"_, 93.

[10]However vague this conclusion seems, Eugene Vinaver did note that "questions in a medieval romance matter more than answers," i.e., that if a question is just raised, it counts for something. ("The Shaping Spirit" 16).

[11]I use the timeline set out by Alexandre Micha in "La Composition de la Vulgate du Merlin," 211-19, as follows:

Arthur's crowning at Pentecost (Spring)
Battle at Bedingran the following January 27
Mordred born ca. March
Yvain leaves home mid-May
Arthur leaves for Benoic June 1
Marriage of Arthur and Guenevere early August
Gathering at Salisbury November 1
Merlin with Viviane end November
(skip eight months)
Rions' challenge in August
Rions killed September

The subsequent chronology is very vague, but approximately two years, five months, have passed up to this point; Micha estimates a total of at least three years, seven months, for the _Merlin_'s events.

[12]_Lancelot_ (Sommer vol. III), 21. We are also given a very different version of Merlin's birth, in which the mother disdains the sight of men and falls victim to a devil's wiles when he promises she need never see him--she is less the unwilling victim. Merlin is brought to Vortigern at the age of twelve, not eight. His deception of Igerne comes about because "il fu de la nature son peire decheuans & deloiaus" (19-21). None of the characteristics presented here fits well with the picture of Merlin in the previous volume, but, as Elspeth Kennedy points out, they do make Viviane, the Lady of the Lake look good. ("The role of the supernatural" 180.)

[13]See Sommer, volume III; Micha, _Lancelot_, volume VII. In her later appearances, she saves Arthur from his own sword, wielded by Accolon; provides a magic ring; cures Lancelot of madness; and creates a magic shield in two parts which unite when Lancelot and Guenevere consummate their love.

[14]There are several versions of Lohot's death in the Arthurian corpus, but he nonetheless always dies well before the Grail quest and the end of Arthur's reign, so he cannot enter into the succession at all. See Sommer, volume II, 316, where he is killed

by Kay; volume III, 159-63, where he becomes mortally ill while imprisoned; and volume VII (Livre d'Artus), 52 and 206-12, where again he is killed by Kay.

[15]Compare the centrality of the incest to events in the Huth, as discussed in Chapter Five.

[16]Merlin interprets a dream of Arthur's, too, while on their way to fight the Romans, which leads into Arthur's defeat of the Giant of Mont St. Michel (428).

[17]Although J.D. Bruce finds the myriad battles in the Merlin boring (I, 463), Micha notes that many recent tactical innovations, especially the mass-strike capability of cavalry, are pictured in the battle scenes. ("Les sources de la Vulgate de Merlin," 309.) This type of presentation likely created a more lively interest which is lost to a modern audience.

[18]It is interesting to note that the archbishop, not a knight, confers knighthood on Arthur. This gives Arthur an additional "consecration" in his kingly task.

[19]Guinebaus, too, sets up a future adventure along the lines of Merlin. He casts an enchantment over a group of revellers in the Perilous Forest in return for a lady's love. Lancelot (implied) will end the enchantment. (244-46)

[21]This "duck hunter," to Arthur's surprise, refers to a buried treasure Arthur thought a secret of his and Merlin's, provoking an amusing dialogue about Merlin's loquaciousness (121).

[22]This ban, while rare in romance, was common in thirteenth-century life. It is enforced here, but does not carry over into the later volumes, implying that the impending battles against the Saxons give an unusual strength to the ban, since the men cannot be "wasted" by in-fighting. Merlin stresses the importance of the ban to Blaise (375). The real-life restrictions were most emphatic for Crusaders and the Knights Templar. (Wilkin 341-43.)

[23]Agravain, even this early, is the grudge-holder of the family and its black sheep. His negative disposition is pictured in the Merlin over pp. 350-58, when Lot and his sons travel north to meet with the rebels. The enmity and attitudes begotten here have significance with regard to later events in the cycle.

[24]Several episodes point to at least a clerical origin; the ban discussed in note 21 above is one, and Wilkin notes (343) that such restrictions were most often urged and imposed by the pope and clergy. The situation leading to Agravain's bitterness is another. While on the embassy to the rebels, the brothers engage in small talk concerning proper and improper wooing; Agravain expresses an

unchivalrous view and is berated by his brothers, especially Gawain, leading to a heated argument. The Knights Templar were supposed to follow a rule which restricted "small talk" in the ranks to avoid just such unnecessary enmities among allies (Wilkin 348-50).

Chapter Five

Magician Beware:
The *Suite du Merlin*

As we move from the Vulgate continuation of *Merlin* to the Huth, we enter yet another variation on the romance species. Of all the works here considered, the Huth *Merlin* perhaps best fulfills traditional romance expectations.[1] However, because the Huth and Vulgate share Robert's base, they share the "historical" emphasis described earlier from Robert, and the religious and legendary expectations raised at the start are thus the same. That fulfillment can take the form of either continuation (and, indeed, others as well[2]) reveals the flexibility of the genre and the fluidity of the legend.

Where the Vulgate cycle's *Merlin* emphasizes the realities of establishing a king's right to his throne through battlefield prowess, the Huth eliminates the necessity for the extended wars pictured in the Vulgate by having Arthur accepted with little opposition, and the controversy over Arthur's birth and birthright is quickly fought out verbally.[3] The differences continue on from there. The post-coronation elements still shared (but not alike in detail) by the two include: Arthur's incest resulting in Mordred; a rebellion by Lot; invasion by Rions; the establishment of future adventures and enchantments; the marriage to Guenevere and return of the Round Table; Arthur's sister and Viviane (Niviene in the Huth) taught by Merlin; and Merlin's enchantment by his lover. We find more diverse fantastic and magical occurrences woven into the fabric, and different plot material as well, as this author is more interested than the Vulgate author in overtly connecting details of events here with those in the future, giving the latter stronger "reasons" for existence.[4]

Merlin in the Huth is as omnipresent as in the Vulgate, but he is less crucial to Arthur's development as king. Merlin loses his roles as mentor and battle advisor, retains his status as prophet and enchanter, and becomes a weaker, perhaps more human, character in the process. To some extent, Merlin's role in these two works parallels that of Arthur; while Arthur is himself militarily active, Merlin is also, but as Arthur settles into the role of courtly "impotence" traditional from Chrétien and the _lais_, Merlin drifts into the background. He is still involved with military excursions in the Huth, but seldom because of Arthur's youth and inexperience. Though Arthur must deal with some battles and invasions, he does so on his own or with the advice of his allies, and Merlin's role consists of stalling or escorting specific knights rather than directing armies in Arthur's name.

The long battles missing, romance _aventures_ do not wait until the final pages to begin. Merlin's place here is with the _chevaliers errants_, not the armies, and his character develops along rather different lines as a result of Arthur's independence.[5] Generally speaking, where the Vulgate takes Merlin into a whole new role when Arthur becomes king, the Huth instead continues the types of activities Merlin performed with Pandragon and Uter, though he must on occasion help Arthur "pick up the pieces" when the young king blunders or stubbornly ignores risks.

The only real remainders of Merlin's fatherly mentor role are found, first, in Arthur's turning to Merlin for advice when the first adventures come to court (I, 175), and second, in Arthur's wedding arrangements, yet even here there are subtle changes. Arthur himself decides, because his barons have complained, that he needs to be married (II, 60). He asks Merlin's advice, and Merlin, agreeing that a king needs a queen, inquires whether Arthur has any preference. Arthur names Gennevre, Leodegan's daughter, as the one he loves, and Merlin at once departs to arrange the marriage. Merlin here plays a "follower" role rather than a "leader", an advisor to Arthur, not a teacher.

The wedding celebrations form the scene for new adventures to come to court. Merlin announces ahead that such adventures are on their way, and it is he who hands out the honors to the three knights (II, 76ff.). This is the only time Merlin directs this kind of action; otherwise, knights are left to request an adventure of the king when it comes, or an adventure comes directly to a particular knight. As might be expected, however, Merlin often gives warning that some adventure is nigh, sometimes hinting at its nature and consequences. Adventures for the knights come either as a result of "assignment"--the king or his surrogate sends a knight out for a particular reason--or as a result of banishment, as with Balin, and, later, Yvain and Gawain. The quests and adventures, as a result, resemble nothing so much as professional necessities or career risks.[6] Adventures generally follow the traditional court-away-court circle we have come to expect in short romances, not the battleground tests of mettle so prevalent in the Vulgate, but the initiative for quests seems no longer to rest with the knights themselves.

As noted above, the historical connections with the Grail history and with British history are still present, and not just in Robert's section. Merlin makes several prophecies about Britain's future, and many about individual knights and geographic places; though Balin's actions lay waste Pelleham's land, for example, Merlin knows that one of the Grail Questers will restore it to health (II, 8). Although these connections with past and future occur, and add to the overall unity, they seem somewhat gratuitous. The series of events connected with the Grail quest are given less gravity, to the extent that it almost seems like just another adventure, not a quest of great religious significance.[7] In keeping with this, Balin's adventures provide a chivalric, human, background to the Quest sequence, which in the Vulgate cycle is left totally divine and proportionately more mysterious.

As mentioned above, magic and fantasy abound in the Huth, and much of it is separate from Merlin. Although Morgain and Niviene are taught by the magician, the magic they perform is their own--especially Morgain's magic, which is predominantly self-centered and inimical to Arthur. The Questing Beast is the first fantastic adventure to come Arthur's way after his coronation, and this marvellous beast, in terms of the narrative, exists solely for the purpose of providing Pellinor and his line with their private _raison d'aventure_. These additional elements parallel the shift in emphasis from Vulgate "epic" to Huth "romance", but they also provide a unique indicator that Arthur (or Britain) at this time has been granted a special mode of existence (Mann 88-89).

Adventures or quests in general are firmly in the romance realm; with the exception of Balin's, they seem to be ends in themselves, self-contained units (though parallels with later events in the cycle often increase their symbolic significance). When compared with the diplomatic excursion of Lot and his sons to the rebels in the Vulgate, only the individual adventures of Balin (as opposed to the excursions prompted by war, like Rions' invasion) successfully go beyond themselves for a clear contribution to a plot progression. (The one exception concerns Arthur's individual excursion which results in the loss of his sword, necessitating a new one; this episode leads to Arthur's acquisition of sword and magic scabbard from the lake, which in itself triggers several plot units.) In this difference, a greater emphasis on thematic unity, as opposed to cause-effect historical unity, can be seen.[8] However, both types of unity are present in both works and do not work to the exclusion of one another. As Morton W. Bloomfield notes, "Life is both rational and irrational. The typical epic stresses the first, the typical romance the second" (108). All adventures, of course, contribute to character development and step-by-step plot movement, but in terms of long-range connections, these mini-romances cannot add up (not that they are meant to) to the epic-historical sweep found in the Vulgate. The effect and, I would argue, the intent are quite different. The Vulgate's crusader ethic gives way here to more courtly chivalric attitudes and follows the shift in the source of unity.

However, the religious element remains strong, and sin in the history of Arthur's reign plays a determining role. Arthur's first acquaintance with Merlin comes the day after the young king's mortal error--the incest with his sister--and Arthur's prophetic dream concerning it. Disguised as a four-year-old, Merlin amazes the king with an interpretation of that dream and warns him about his sin, but Arthur refuses to believe the child and sends him off. When Merlin returns as an old man and gives Arthur the same information, the king is more willing to accept it, but still amazed at the stranger's knowledge. When Merlin reveals both the king's parentage and his own identity, Arthur's skepticism is slowly replaced by the true knowledge of his sin. At several points later in the work, Merlin reminds Arthur of this burden, and his tone each time emphasizes Arthur's human equality with others (as king, he should not judge others' sins so harshly when he himself is weak) and the fatal consequences that one sin can have (cf. II, 66). Merlin repeatedly drums into Arthur the fact of his sin, where in the Vulgate it is quickly passed over, and brings out to the reader as well as to Arthur the significance of this sin in the events to come.

Indeed, Arthur's incest sets off the chain of events which will cause Britain's fall. (As Fanni Bogdanow points out, this helps to reduce the role of Lancelot and Guenevere in the post-Vulgate cycle. Romance 142-44.) Merlin presents the king with two prophecies concerning his future, but does not overtly connect them. First, a child born the following May will wreak great destruction in Britain and cause it to be left without a king. Second, Arthur's incest will result in great trouble for the realm. Arthur takes steps to destroy the unknown child who is supposed to destroy him, but Merlin refuses to reveal which child, thereby refusing to sanction this course, as a good Christian should. It is lucky that Arthur does not make the connection between the two, since it would be easy to track down his sister's child. Merlin refuses to identify the child because to aid Arthur in destroying it would endanger his own soul.

> "Sire," fait Merlins, "[je cuit bien] que li descouvrirs vaurroit meius, qui vaurroit garder au preu de la terre. Mais quel chose que la terre i gaaignast, jou i perderoie trop. Car je i perderoie l'ame de moi, dont il m'est ore plus que de tout che pais. Et pour chou le vous celerai jou. Je voel mieus m'ame sauver que la terre." (I, 159)

Merlin clearly knows the divine plan for the future and cannot take action to avert it without defying God. Merlin elsewhere is reluctant to discuss in too great detail things which he prophesies. He tells Arthur, "je ne vous descouverroie en nulle maniere les choses que li haus maistres a establies a sa volente" (II, 131). His attitude here is consistent with the role he played earlier with Pandragon and Uter. Although Merlin may have known beforehand and been able to prevent Arthur's incest, as he here is able (but unwilling) to prevent the child of doom from maturing, Merlin has consistently maintained the path set for him and his talents by God even when it meant a personal loss, as with the death of Pandragon. Merlin's character in the Huth is rather more self-centered than in the Vulgate, but he does not make the mistake of reverting to his demonic side. Merlin's God-given talents are directed towards advancing the realm toward the Grail quest, and this religious duty takes precedence over secular loyalties. Where the secular will not interfere with the religious, Merlin's loyalty to Arthur is clear, but not totally unselfish, as I will discuss below.

Arthur's unwitting sin (incest) and his known sin (adultery with Lot's wife) converge and affect his kingdom. When Arthur takes steps to destroy the child Merlin prophesied, he has all the children born in a three-week span collected and brought to him. Initially, he plans to kill them there, but ends by putting them all on an unpiloted ship and leaving their death to God; God, however, saves the children. The child Lot sent, thinking it his own son, was shipwrecked by itself before ever reaching the king and is brought up elsewhere. Meanwhile, Lot believes that his son has been killed and rebels against Arthur by taking his army to join the invasion by Rions. Merlin goes to Lot and explains the boy is alive, but Lot doesn't believe him and attacks Arthur's army. The rebellion of Lot is not justified for the reasons that Lot expresses, but it is justified for reasons he is unaware of--Arthur's adultery with Lot's wife. Arthur here repeats his father's sin, but the difference in the two events crucially affects the respective results. Only Merlin and Arthur (and probably the woman) know the full circumstances, however, and Arthur is not held accountable for Lot's death[9] (just as Uter was not for the Duke's death).

The other barons whose children actually were on the ship had been reconciled with Arthur earlier when Merlin came and told them the true fate of the children and, obscurely, Arthur's reasons for this deed (I, 211). Had Merlin not been able to assure the barons of their children's safety, Arthur would have had more trouble on his hands, on a scale similar to the rebellions in the Vulgate (but note the widely divergent motives). Here, however, Merlin manages to avert rebellion: "Ensi acorda Merlins le roi as ses barons, si em peust grant mal estre avenu ou pais, si Merlins n'i eust mise cest[e] acorde (I, 212)." Arthur remains ignorant of the children's fate until later, but Merlin eventually tells him, at the same time revealing that the one crucial child was not among them anyway, and is himself safe (II, 139). Merlin again acts as protector, here protecting Arthur from full-scale rebellion and from a timely attack by Lot. The incest, of course, was done in ignorance (although Arthur must have known it to be adultery), but the wholesale murder of children would be totally unacceptable in a king, as its overt echoes of Herod's Slaughter indicate. God's favor for Arthur (or perhaps more likely, for Britain) is reinforced by His action of saving the children, paralleling Merlin's efforts on other fronts.

The central episode in the Huth presents the story of Balin and the origin of the Grail wasteland.[10] Balin is a poor knight, but proves to be the "best" in a typical romance test--he unties a knot which only the best knight in the realm can untie. After proving his worth, however, he initiates a chain of events which ends in the deaths of Balin himself and his brother. Although warned not to keep the sword which the knot held, he chooses wrongly not to give it up.

> Et li chevaliers dist que l'espee ne rendera il pas, s'il en devoit estre tenus a vilains de tous chiaus de la court. "et je vous di," fait elle, "que se vous l'em portes qu'il vous en mal averra. Car bien sachies que li hom que vous primes en ochirres sera li hom ou monde que vous plus ames.[11] . . . Ore le portes, se il vous plaist, que bien sachies que vous em portes vostre mort avoecques vous." Et cil li dist que se la mors i devoit estre, si l'em porteroit il, car trop li samble l'espee boine et biele. (I, 217)

We learn later (I, 223-24) that this "test" originated from an unhealthy desire for vengeance and is set in motion for evil ends. For Arthur's court, the test serves a double purpose. First, it reveals that the virtue of Arthur's court is not all it may seem. Arthur, guilty of several sins, himself fails to untie the knot where he succeeded before, while innocent, in a crucial "test by sword." Second, it implies that Balin's "accursed" path once he decides to keep the sword will work to the detriment of Arthur's realm. The theme of human vengeance as wrong attaches itself to Balin, climaxing in his use of "la Lanche Vengeresse" and his death sent him by God "pour le fait que vous fesistes chies le roi Pellehan en lieu de venganche, si n'est mie la venganche si grans comme li fais le requesist" (II, 47).

Merlin follows Balin through most of his adventures and tries several times to warn the knight away from the path to Pelleham's castle. All these warnings are in vain, reinforcing Balin's continued willfulness and desire for vengeance against the invisible knight as well as pointing up Merlin's inability to control events totally. This inability is not his weakness, but rather emphasizes the human weaknesses of the other characters.

In Balin's story a major difference in Merlin's Huth role can be seen. In the Vulgate every non-rebel seemed to follow Merlin's advice, whether he was disguised or not. The impression is left that Merlin would not bother trying were his advice not to be taken. Here, though, many people ignore Merlin's advice, and always to their disadvantage. Balin goes on, lays waste to Pelleham's land, and kills Balan, his brother; Arthur is nearly killed and loses his first sword; Lot refuses to listen and is killed. Conversely, when Merlin's advice is followed such people benefit, even Balin, who captures King Rions with Merlin's aid.

However, the tightly predestined nature of the Vulgate is in large part due to Merlin's direction of events. Here, although he issues warnings of what will happen, the people seem to be more free to go their own way, to create avoidable problems. Though this "free will" is qualified by the omniscient narrator's predictions and Merlin's miscellaneous inscriptions and prophecies,[12] the impression remains that a clear chain of events is involved. If a knight follows path A instead of path B, the future is directed from path A; but the knight still had the initial choice. The effect is rather Boethian, in that destiny or fate plays a paramount role, but destiny is formed by chance events along the chain of possibilities (Mann 86-87). Essentially, adventures come from God, but the choices from men. Mischance, Bogdanow states, rather than Fortune, is the directing force here, though she seems to miss the point that men's reactions to mischance are more important in interpreting events (Romance 148-50).

To some extent, Merlin's less-than-total success at directing events in the Huth is consistent with his portrayal here. He is capable of serving his own interests as well as Arthur's. We see an instance of this when Morgain[13] first tries to substitute forgeries for Arthur's magic sword and scabbard. She has been entrusted with the originals and wants to give them to her lover to keep him safe, but she confuses the imitation and the real ones. When the knight is badly wounded, he tells Arthur, untruthfully, that Morgain plotted this way to kill the king (though she later will do just this, in earnest). Morgain asks Merlin's help in calming Arthur's anger against her, and Merlin agrees to reconcile the two; though he engages in no direct lies in doing so, he hides Morgain's very real betrayal of her brother's trust (I, 267-71). Blame is to some extent mitigated in that Merlin had warned Arthur before (I, 265) to keep close tabs on the scabbard. Arthur, of course, has no reason to distrust his sister at this point, and her unsisterly betrayal due to her illicit affair mirrors other sins with similar negative consequences throughout the narrative.

Merlin had previously taught Morgain much of his art--though she was skilled to some extent before (I, 120)--because he had fallen in love with her. At that time she was pregnant with Yvain, and once the child was born, Morgain sent Merlin away to avoid being compromised. Although this relationship was present in the Vulgate, its ramifications are much more serious here, as Morgain is not sent from court (or killed) now, due to Merlin's intervention, though she certainly grows to hate her brother and becomes a dangerous enemy to him. One can easily excuse Merlin his actions by attributing them to his foreknowledge and unwillingness to avert God's will, but on the surface his integrity is clearly compromised. In this way, Merlin shares the common downfall of others in the Huth--lust is the indicator, with Merlin, Morgain, and Arthur, that all is not well with that character.

His relationship with Niviene, too, is different. Again, she is not openly antagonistic toward Merlin, but here, in her thoughts, she reveals fear and near-loathing. When he first teaches her his magic, she is a willing and able student, but, like Morgain, she wishes to dispense with him once she has learned all she wants. Unlike Morgain, however, she is not married and does not have the clear excuse to send him away. She also underestimates Merlin's affection for her, for when her father sends for her she does ask Merlin if he wants to come along, thinking that he would not leave Arthur's court--but he does, and secretly, since he knows Arthur would not give him congé (II, 142).

Merlin's reputation among women in this work is very negative and is always tied to his demonic heritage (which is openly discussed in this work). Although Ygerne is stated earlier to have died, when it becomes necessary to prove Arthur's identity she comes to court, very much alive. In an extended scene, Merlin (still in disguise from his first meeting with Arthur earlier) has Uter's men present their evidence concerning the child conceived at Tintagel. Ygerne is asked to corroborate, and she does so, blaming Merlin for taking her child away for his own diabolic purposes. She openly accuses Merlin of destroying the child, citing his demonic blood as a major factor in his planning:

> Car le premier enfant que Dieus nous ot envoiiet emporta [Merlin], si ne sai qu'il en fist, si moustra bien qu'il estoit estrait (dou dyable) d'anemi, quant il ne vaut mie tant attendre que li enfes fust crestiiens, ains l'emporta anchois qu'il eust rechut baptesme, pour chou que il ne voloit mie que Dieus euust part en la creature. (I, 169)

Of course, Merlin proves that the child he took then is now in fact the young king, and great joy erupts in the palace as Arthur's identity as Uter's son becomes clear. This type of suspicion over Merlin's motives appears only in jealous courtiers in the Vulgate, and such people are always emphatically characterized as "bad."

Merlin's shape-changing abilities meet greater acceptance here, perhaps because he is widely known as a devil's son. He goes to no trouble to hide his "methods" from the court; when, during the course of hearing evidence on Arthur's birth, it becomes necessary for Merlin to assume his usual form, he does so--without leaving the room (I, 169) as he always did in the Vulgate. He uses disguise at several points later in the narrative, usually to give anonymous help to Arthur's knights. However, with Arthur, Merlin is never disguised after this first encounter, and his playful shape-changing done earlier with Uter and Pandragon disappears.

Later in the narrative, another woman brings up Merlin's demonic background in accusing him of self-interest when he reveals that her eldest son, Tor, is not her husband's.

> Merlins, or voi ja bien que vous n'estes mie dou tout de la maniere as autres dyables. Che savons nous que li autre(s) dyable(s) vaurroi[en]t tous jours que li pechi[e] de chascun fuissent repost et cele, si que il n'en issist ja de la bouce au pecheour, se che n'estoit par gap et par eschar, et vous voles que jou descuevre le mien; si le descoverrais, mais sachies que la Dieus ne vous en savra gret; car vous ne le faites mie pour l'amour de [Dieu] ne pour moi amender, fors pour moustrer vostre savoir. (II, 133)

It is, of course, in the son's interest to know he is a king's son, and Merlin's tactics seem justified; he even comments that the gentility of Tor's father makes the situation no shame to either the woman or her son (II, 72). It is interesting to note that only women bring up Merlin's demonic connection; Niviene will use it later as an excuse to fear him and to rid herself of him. The men show little interest in this parentage, perhaps because they fear him less or feel less vulnerable to a devil's trickery.

These accusations, repeated as they are, certainly serve as reminders about Merlin's "blood," and the narrative reveals a belief in blood showing true, as with Tor. Merlin does show himself to be less altruistic here than in the Vulgate text; he comments several times that he performs certain actions in order to be remembered. Still, he is no worse than other men in the narrative, and certainly better than some. He continues to be ideologically against <u>maleficium</u>, as demonstrated by the episode with the two harper-enchanters.[14] These two have set themselves up in a forest, and any who hear their music will come under their control. Merlin knows this and stops his ears to avoid being overcome himself so he can end their evildoing. Note that he is susceptible to their magic although he possesses the foreknowledge to avoid it and the superior magic to destroy them. He performs his magic in such a way that these evil magicians will remain subdued until Arthur's reign is over, at which time they will revive, so he is working here for Arthur's benefit. After he finishes this task, though, he clearly states that he wants to be remembered for his work:

> Et certes se je cuidaisse longement vivre, je ne m'en(en)tremesisse ja de tel chose, car asses moustraisse de mon sens a mon vivant. Mais je sai bien que a morir me vouvient prochainnement, et pour chou ai je fait si grant miervelle que je voel que elle soit apres ma mort tiesmoing et demoustranche de men grant savoir. (II, 158)

Merlin's "grant savoir", of course, is in itself a demonstration of God's power, but this expression above reveals more earthly than divine concerns. Since this is his last action prior to being entombed, our high impression of his motives is compromised here, as it is with his behavior with Morgain and Niviene and with his final attitude to his death.

During their stay in Brittany, Merlin reveals to Niviene that he knows the manner of his death and that someone was plotting it even then. She, of course, is concerned to learn if her spells to hide her plans work so that he cannot tell who is plotting. Merlin's attitude is not as accepting, nor as knowledgeable, as in the Vulgate. Earlier, Merlin had told Arthur of his shameful death and that only with God's consent could it be averted (I, 178).

While with Niviene, Merlin sees that Arthur is in danger (whether from the war with the five kings or from Morgain is unclear), but he delays telling her and delays returning. When she reproaches him, he explains that his reluctance to leave Brittany is related to his approaching death:

> [J]e laisse a estre en la grant Bretaigne pour deus choses: l'une si est pour l'amour de vous, car je vous aimme tant que je ne porroie pas sans vous demourer; l'autre raison si [est que je] me tieng hors pour chou que mes sors me dist que ja n'i serai si tost venus que on me fera morir ou par puison ou par autre chose." "Coument!" fait elle, "et ne vous en poes vous garder?" "Nennil," fait il, "car je cui ja si enchantes que je ne sai ki ceste mort m'apareille." "Voles vous," fait elle, "savoir si grant partie des choses a venir et si estes ore a che menes que vous en aves perdu la scienche?" "Encore," fait il, "en sai jou grant partie de celles qui n'apartienent a ma vie ne a ma mort. Mais des moies choses sui je si contrabatus par enchantemens que je n'i sai metre conseil, car les enchantemens qui sont fait ne puis je desfaire se je ne voel m'arme perdre; mais certes mieus vaurroie je que mes cors fust tornes a honte par auchune traison que l'ame de moi fust perdue." (II, 151-52)

This Merlin is much more human, with typical human weaknesses, than the figure drawn in the Vulgate. The unhappy end to his love is foreshadowed by the two stories he tells Niviene about Dyane (II, 146-48) and Anasteu (II, 193), in which both male lovers are entombed, Dyane's alive. Some pity for Merlin's situation is aroused by these tales, as it is too when Baudemagus tries in vain to free the magician four days later (II, 198). Merlin, too, is coming to Arthur's aid, however reluctantly, so our opinion of his end depends to some extent on how we interpret his last attempt to help the king. Still, Merlin is now gone, and Niviene assumes his role as Arthur's protector, saving the king from Morgain's plot using Accolon and from the magic mantle as the narrative closes.

Although in the Vulgate Merlin occasionally leaves Arthur to get himself out of trouble and fight his own wars near the end, this "abandonment" has been prepared for there. Arthur has been taught by Merlin, his nephews and other allies have matured, and the author slowly withdraws Merlin from the director's chair. In the Huth, the abandonment is more sudden, lacking any preparation or farewell. As a result, Merlin appears to be more selfish and callous; as mentioned above, his role as mentor (substitute father) is missing in the Huth, and this role seemed to endow him with a more caring, fatherly attitude toward Arthur and his court.

And what of Blaise? Merlin still has him writing his book, as begun in Robert's base text, but finds the Northumberland retreat unnecessary. On his first visit after Arthur's coronation, Merlin asks Blaise to relocate to Camelot and continue his work there. Blaise does, and several references are made to Merlin providing Blaise there with new material to record. Generally, less is made of the book and its scribe than in the Vulgate; the attention is instead given to recording the various adventures of Arthur's knights--fifty scribes are set to that task. These small details reflect much about the Huth's priorities. Merlin's historical book is less important (or less interesting) than the romance adventures; in the same way, the Grail itself is less important than the people and events surrounding it, like Balin's tragic story.

Also, Blaise plays an even smaller role in the Huth continuation, for Merlin does not use him, as he does in the Vulgate, as a confidant. Much of what we know about Merlin as a "private" person in the Vulgate comes from his conversations with Blaise, especially when Merlin talks about his relationship with Viviane and its end. Here, Merlin doesn't even say good-bye to Blaise (or to Arthur, for that matter). This further reduction in Blaise's already minor role mirrors both the author's priorities in reference to the Grail's religious import and the reduced concern with Merlin's achievements and personality. Arthur exhibits no concern over the magician's disappearance here and sends no knights to seek his friend.

The Huth continuation contains numerous infelicities and inconsistencies, but the narrative's overall impact is not seriously weakened. This portrayal of Arthur's court revolves around the repeated sins of its members. While we are given clear indications of God's "presence" in the realm, both through Merlin and through such actions as preventing the death of the May-born children, neither of these is sufficient to control the paths of the knights, king included. Each person suffers from the inability to make correct choices; even when alternatives are offered or warnings are given, these people all too often choose the wrong path. Merlin himself is not immune. Although lust is traditionally the devil's own characteristic, Merlin here shares this sin with his fully human counterparts, while he resists several other opportunities to endanger his soul. The battle between good and evil, suggested from the beginning by the council of devils, is ongoing. Galahad will come and remedy some of the damage we see done in the narrative--Merlin prepares the way for him (II, 59-60) and the Grail Quest--but Galahad is powerless to redirect the free, sinful, individuals of the court, his primary task in this cycle being to heal the Maimed King, not to achieve the _visio Dei_ (Bogdanow, _Romance_ 137).

All Merlin does is with the ultimate goal of the Quest; that is the task is he given in Robert's story and both continuations carry that forward. Merlin is given the power from God to further that goal and he cannot undermine it--not without endangering his soul. Merlin is not God's proxy but His tool, and that relationship is clearer in the Huth than the Vulgate because Merlin's weaknesses are given greater play. The theme of sin's ramifications in the Huth comes across especially strong because Merlin himself, perhaps the individual closest to God in Arthur's court, is vulnerable. If we can safely interpolate the "Dolorous Stroke" section from the Cambridge manuscript (which unfortunately has not been published in full) into the lacuna in the Huth, Merlin reveals that his "divine" knowledge is unimpaired, though his power is limited. Merlin cannot enter the sacred chamber which Balin trespassed. A White Monk must assume "the arms of Jesus Christ" (i.e., vest himself for mass) before he, alone, can enter the room safely and remove the wounded and unconscious men inside (Bogdanow, _Romance_ 248-49).

Merlin, unlike the monk, knows what has been and must be done and knows the "rules" for entering the room, but he cannot do it himself. He is powerless to act here at the castle, powerless to prevent his death, powerless to forestall several tragic deeds in spite of his superior knowledge--all because he does act in accord with God's will.

Although Britain suffers, it does so "legitimately," because of its sins. Much of the tragedy arises from our awareness that much good, alongside sin, is present in these people, and their major fault is purely in being human. Merlin gives an indirect indication of this relationship as he compares the suffering due to Balin's upcoming disobedience to that resulting from Eve's disobedience.

The parallel between the narrative theme and Merlin's portrayal is well drawn. While Merlin's end through his lady's magic is consistent in both continuations, the difference in details is crucial. In the Vulgate, Merlin knows, accepts, and prepares for his imprisonment. His stature is retained and God's will through Viviane is played out with calm dignity and no trace of enmity. In the Huth, Merlin balks. He tries to avoid the inevitable, playing for time and creating monuments to his own "grant savoir." At the end, he is left to die, rather than merely left alone and granted occasional visits from his lady. Unlike Viviane, Niviene must resort to violence to rid herself of this unwelcome devil's son once and for all. The divergence of the two portrayals reflects the approach of each work. Christian and pagan fighting over the land of Britain puts the societal approach to the religious movement of the narrative foremost in the Vulgate. In the Huth, the personal religious life, the sin and the sinner, receives the emphasis, and here Merlin is not the omniscient mentor leading king and country to peace but one of the kingdom of sinners.

Notes - Chapter Five

1 Fanni Bogdanow describes the difference as "the Vulgate is little more than a chronicle of Arthur's wars against the rebel kings and the Saxons, [while] the *Suite du Merlin* is an Arthurian romance in the proper sense" (*Romance* 28). I disagree with the assessment of the Vulgate, but that there is a dichotomy between the two is clear.

2 The *Livre d'Artus* (Volume 7 of Sommer's *Vulgate Version*) and the *Perlesvaus* are among these other continuations.

3 The Cambridge ms. of the Suite is different in that it retains the rebellion of the kings, but resembles the Huth ms. more than the Vulgate otherwise. (See Bogdanow, "Rebellion" 17.) The Cambridge ms. is generally accepted as Malory's source (Vinaver, "La Genese" 300). All references here are to the Huth ms., edited in two volumes by Gaston Paris and Jacob Ulrich; citations in the text are given by volume and page.

4 Vinaver points out, for example, that Arthur's sword Excalibur here comes from the lake, therefore giving it a reason to return to the lake in the *Mort* ("La Genèse" 297).

5 Zumthor, while noting Merlin's new role, goes overboard in saying there is nothing of the historical prophet left of Merlin in this work (*Merlin le Prophète* 201).

6 R. Morris comments that the Suite's attitude to adventure is negative, a discipline instead of a pleasure, and that even Arthur defends the state through the means of adventure instead of neglecting the state to seek adventure (*Character* 88).

7 The Vulgate *Queste* is, in Bogdanow's words, the "triumph of heavenly over earthly chivalry," and the post-Vulgate *Queste* "a chapter in the story of Logres" (*Romance* 203). See her final chapter in *Romance* for further discussion of what she calls "The New Arthuriad."

8 In several places in her book on the post-Vulgate cycle, Bogdanow overstates the Vulgate's lack of unity as compared to the newer creation. I would argue rather that the unity is based upon different principles.

9 My conclusions about this episode coincide with those of Bogdanow in "Rebellion" 12-13.

10 Bogdanow in *Romance* prints the Cambridge ms. version of the Dolorous Stroke which the Huth ms. lacks, pages 241-49; Vinaver's edition of Malory also contains a smaller excerpt on pages 1315-16.

[11]There is some confusion as to whether this is actually true, since Balin seems to lose the sword at Pelleham's castle. See Vinaver, Rise of Romance, Chapter Four.

[12]Both Zumthor and Bloomfield comment on the romance's tendency to replace what we see as normal cause-and-effect with either "the divine center" or magic. (Bloomfield 113; Zumthor, Essai 138.)

[13]The name "Morgain" alternates in the text with "Morgue", but the same person is clearly meant.

[14]Zumthor, Merlin le Prophète, compares this episode to Merlin's earlier defeat of Vortigern's magicians (232), and I agree that both indicate an alignment against misuse of magic.

Chapter Six

Conclusion:
Malory's *Le Morte Darthur*

Although two hundred years passed from the French cycles to Malory, nothing substantive happened to Merlin in that time. The cycles continued to be popular, and several adaptations appeared in English, though none of these was a thorough reconstruction along new imaginative lines as Malory's was to be.[1] I do not intend to cover all angles on Malory's use of the supernatural,[2] or even Merlin in particular, but I will bring in some ideas which grow from the previous chapters to serve as a focal point for summarizing my conclusions.

But first I need to comment on Malory's portrait and use of Merlin in "The Tale of King Arthur."[3] Because Merlin is present only in the first of Malory's tales, most of my discussion will involve only that section, just as in the previous chapters I bring in the later sections of the French cycles rarely. Again, in proceeding this way I do not want to give the impression that I see any of these works as totally independent of its respective cycle, but rather that each is a coherent unit responsive to independent evaluation alongside the larger picture.

Malory begins his history of Britain with the circumstances of Arthur's conception. We start with the fact that Uther is king; Merlin appears, with no explanation of who or what he is, at the seige of Tintagel to help Uther into Igrayne's bed. The ruse to enter Tintagel involves no magic herbs, and Malory makes a point of killing the Duke before Arthur is conceived so the future king is technically not adulterous issue. Merlin's background is never told, but he is accepted from the beginning as an advisor by Uther, the barons, and the archbishop, so we must assume that Merlin's history has preceded him. However, because we have no stated background to draw judgements from, we must depend on the picture Malory draws of Merlin from the time he helps Uther.

This picture of Merlin is basically positive.[4] He helps Uther; he establishes Arthur's right to the throne by occasioning Uther's deathbed declaration; he advises the archbishop with regard to protecting Arthur once he pulls the sword; he provides strategic advice during the northern kings' rebellion. Arthur, however, establishes his reign without Merlin's supernatural help, relying rather on the martial aid of his loyal barons.

All this time, the facts of Arthur's birth are unknown. When the northern kings rebel, Merlin reveals to them Arthur's parentage; some kings doubt him, calling Merlin a "wytche" and a "dreme-reder" (18), but their negative assessment must be weighed against their rebellion, and we know that Merlin speaks true. The next scene provides an immediate contrast, when the loyal barons in Arthur's encampment follow Merlin's advice, and confirm his reliability.

The shape-shifting, "automatic" travel and magical aid we saw in the Vulgate's rebellion section are missing. Merlin is, as in Geoffrey, a master of disguise and a prophet, and, as in the Vulgate, a strategist, but Arthur makes his own decisions and wins his own battles in this section (i.e., without anyone's supernatural feats), so Merlin's role is placed well below that of Arthur. The king, not his advisor, is the center of attention.

In the same sense, Merlin does not serve as the keeper of Arthur's morals. First, Arthur has a liaison with the visiting Lionors and begets a son (38). Then Arthur and Lot's wife "were agreed" to have an affair during her visit to Carlyon. This second affair, while adulterous, at first might be mitigated by the narrator's statement that she was sent as a spy (41). The problem, of course, is that she not only is Lot's wife, but (unknown to either) also Arthur's half-sister; Arthur's lecherous leanings, relatively innocent in his first affair, get him in trouble with the second. Merlin appears soon after and reveals to Arthur his birth and his incest, informing him that as punishment from God the son of this incest will destroy him and his realm (44).

Is this sin of Arthur's Merlin's fault? An interesting comment from Ulphin raises this possibility. When Igrayne comes to court to affirm Arthur's parentage, Ulphin accuses her of treason because she hid Arthur's birth: he claims she has caused the king's misfortunes because (he thinks) the rebels are unaware of Arthur's high birth. When Igrayne reveals the full circumstances, Ulphin shifts this blame to Merlin, but the accusation is dropped as the reunion of mother and son takes center stage (45-46). While Ulphin may not know of the incest, his righteous accusation, wrong in his assumption of the rebels' ignorance, still carries weight with regard to _Arthur's_ ignorance. In this sense, Merlin is the cause of the king's misfortunes since he possessed the knowledge which could have prevented Arthur's incest. I see the blame as shared equally, however, between Merlin and Arthur--had Arthur not committed adultery, his ignorance would not have hurt him.

The emphasis on Arthur's adultery is appropriate, I think, because it, rather than the shipwreck of the children as in the Suite, later fuels Lot's rebellion and causes his death, and other adulterous liaisons also have negative effects on the kingdom. The May Day episode reinforces Arthur's guilt; in Malory, all the children but Mordred die. Although Malory states that many of the parents blamed Merlin more than Arthur, the plan is Arthur's, and the guilt is his. "[F]or drede and for love" of Arthur (56), the parents keep peace, and blaming Merlin allows them to do this more easily. Arthur shows himself particularly willful later, too, when Merlin directly warns him not to marry Guenevere, but Arthur is in love and refuses to take the advice offered him (97). From the beginning, Arthur is pictured as politically, martially, and personally independent of Merlin, taking or leaving advice as it suits him. Arthur's decisions are his personal responsibility, and their consequences devolve directly upon the king, not Merlin.

While Merlin does perform some magic--in saving Arthur's life and setting up some "marvels"--the first mention of any demonic connection appears just as Nyneve is about to enter the picture. His knowledge has been gained, one knight says, "by the devylles craffte" (118).[5] Still, it is that very knowledge that Nyneve wants; she shows Merlin "good chere" until she learns all she wants, and he dotes on her all the more because of it (125). So, in a way, she brings her problem onto herself, while still fearing him because he is a devil's son. Although Merlin is a possibly fearful being, until Nyneve's presence in the narrative his aid to Arthur and his knights is all positive. And, while Merlin's loss could harm Arthur, Nyneve proves herself a sufficient substitute and a suitable opponent for Morgan.[6] The change in Merlin can be accounted for in two ways; first, Nyneve needs to be portrayed positively, and second, Merlin is being punished, on the principle of _contrappasso_, for his earlier deception of Igrayne.[7]

Why did Malory change and reduce Merlin's role? The answer to this question is thorny, as it reflects upon the entire thematic concern of the work. Generations of Malory scholarship have put forward interpretations, some complementary and some polar. These have ranged from Larry Benson's emphasis on the balance achieved in the first tale[8] by eliminating Merlin's background, to emphasis placed on various human, historical or political themes by eliminating the supernatural themes imposed by Merlin.[9] While it is not my purpose to attempt a definitive reading, some comments can and should be made concerning how I see Merlin affecting the narrative.

I can, for example, certainly accept that by eliminating Merlin's Grail prophecies in Book I Malory has postponed any real concern with the Grail for his sixth tale (Moorman 69; Pochoda 88), but his treatment of the theme in the first tale implies more than simple postponement or "de-interlacing." The Round Table is in no way connected to Joseph's table or the Last Supper; its ownership history still moves from Uther to Lodegreauns to Arthur, but its significance begins from Arthur's acquisition. The chivalry connected with it is Arthur's creation, and the names Merlin "founde" on the seats are current occupants, Arthur's men. The two exceptions, of course, look forward to the Grail quest, but Merlin discourages discussion of the empty seats (102).

As the narrative continues, this lack of religious history in connecting Arthur's reign with Joseph and the Grail places the king in the same position that his incest does, outside legitimate religious lines. Britain is a Christian kingdom, and Arthur's miraculous accession by the sword in the stone revealed God's favor, but the un-Christian behavior of the kingdom's ruler leads to his downfall. The withdrawal of God's favor is symbolically revealed in Arthur's rash attempt to avenge Gryfflet's honor. Arthur fights Pellinor and would have been killed had not Merlin cast a spell--Arthur's sword had broken, the sword he removed from the stone (51-52). This occurs after the incest and before the May Day children die, so the death of the children (and the concomitant survival of Mordred) is yet another indication of Arthur's distance from God. Merlin can provide another sword for Arthur, but it is not one given by God. And Merlin cannot revive the boatload of dead infants. Arthur continues on as king for many years, of course, but Merlin has already announced his execution and it only awaits the maturity of the executioner chosen by God.

The troubles caused by Arthur's new sword and its magic scabbard also indicate in several ways that Arthur is the cause of his own problems. First, Merlin warns Arthur several times to keep the scabbard, which prevents serious injury, close to him (54, 78, 125), but instead Arthur entrusts it to his sister, Morgan (78). While Morgan at first has given her brother no reason to distrust her, Arthur has stretched the advice Merlin gave him in order, it seems, to remove the burden of "keeping" it from his own shoulders. Second, when Arthur received the sword, he promised to grant the Lady a boon (53), placing himself under unrestricted obligation to her. The unrestricted promise is an old romance sign for trouble (see Chrétien's Charrette, for example), and the sign shows true, though the path is convoluted. When the Lady asks Arthur for either the death of Balin or the maiden who brought Balin's sword, Balin kills the Lady to avenge his mother's death (65-66). This action leads into Balin's adventures which culminate in the Dolorous Stroke, a signal blight on Arthur's kingdom which can be "cured" only by the spiritual Galahad. Arthur's sword and scabbard cause repeated trouble, and the intricate line of causation can be traced, symbolically at least, to Arthur himself.[10]

Much of the change in Merlin's role, then, results in heightened emphasis on Arthur. Since the French cycles (especially the Vulgate) place Merlin in a superior role to the kings and gradually withdraw the magician, immediately subordinating Merlin reverses the roles we have come to expect. One can see in this either a return to Geoffrey's emphasis on Arthur's blame, a negative portrayal of an ineffectual ruler, or a greater concern with political or social than with religious or spiritual conditions.

Whichever (or even all of the above), the focus in Malory's first, and last, tale is on Arthur. The intervening material illustrates the effects of Arthur's decisions on other people more than on the king, but the final tale returns to the man who, due to his position, has doomed others along with himself.

With the emphasis shifted to Arthur, to politics instead of religion, what remains for Merlin? I see him functioning in a very similar way to Geoffrey's Merlin, but without the ambiguities. Merlin points out weaknesses in the king and the chivalric code; he provides a sense of unity through prophetic words and deeds; and he is a figure of authority, given weight by his association with the divine. Each of these functions deserves examination.

The weaknesses of the king are for the most part discussed above. Arthur's chivalry is condemned through a long series of interconnected events, encompassing eventually the entire narrative. The events surrounding Balin and his sword will serve as an example. Balin first comes into possession of the sword by means of a test very similar to Arthur's; "the best knight" will be able to release the sword from its scabbard. Arthur tries and is unsuccessful (this is after the incest). Balin's first act with the sword is to behead the Lady who provided Arthur Excalibur, an act of revenge committed while the Lady is under Arthur's protection. This action, which Merlin will essentially forgive Balin, precipitates Lanceor's death in defense of Arthur's honor, leading to his lady Columbe's death, which Merlin mysteriously connects with the upcoming Dolorous Stroke. This chain of events illustrates the chaos which results when personal vengeance is allowed to take precedence over social order. The chain, too, can be traced back to Arthur's attempt to avenge Gryfflet's honor by fighting Pellinor. The code of chivalry Arthur institutes after these events take place attempts to control individual impulses. The code, however, tries to sustain the group at the expense of individuality, and this is one of its failures. There is no impulse for growth, only for stagnating stability.[11]

Once Balin has died, killing his brother with the sword, Merlin takes the sword, puts a new pommel on it and prepares it in an anvil to await Galahad. The test for Galahad's sword again echoes that of Arthur, but this time Arthur does not attempt it, perhaps having learned his inadequacies. Galahad, of course, succeeds in reversing the damage done by Balin, symbolically showing the superiority of divine over seigneurial inspiration, since even Lancelot, the best "earthly" knight, cannot succeed by following his chivalric code of behavior. This superiority is again implied when the same sword (Balin's and Galahad's) is used later by Lancelot to kill Gawain--we have essentially returned to the chaos of the world of Balin. Arthur's chivalry meets with limited, purely secular, success, as symbolized by Arthur's death--it is a "worshipfull dethe" (as Merlin predicts), by chivalric standards, but it signals the parallel death of those very standards and the underlying cause is Arthur's failure on the spiritual level. Elizabeth Pochoda, in fact, sees that lack of a spiritual dimension to Arthur's code of chivalry as one reason for the collapse of the system (Pochoda 110).[12] Galahad uses, literally, the same tools other knights have, but his priorities are different, and his religious priorities echo those of Merlin.

Each time Merlin issues a prophecy, it concerns events crucial to the thematic development of the narrative. As Ben Fiester noticed, the prophecies at Lot's death are arranged in order of increasing seriousness, beginning with Merlin's death, moving to the Dolorous Stroke, to Morgan's betrayal, to Mordred's rebellion (30). By its very nature, prophecy provides unity to the narrative, but it also--due to the authority vested in Merlin--points to thematic concerns by underlining the importance of events which reveal theme.

Merlin is given authority by several means. First, although Malory as narrator does not intrude judgements into the text but allows his characters that function, Malory is the ultimate source of authority, represented by Merlin (among others) in the text. Within the narrative, Merlin's connection with God, revealed by his ability to make Uther speak ("God and I will make him speak," Merlin says, 11), and his working relationship with the Archbishop of Canterbury provide him with divine authority which is voiced in his prophetic gift. Merlin's infallibility, which the reader can see proven over time, is connected with the divine source. Also, Merlin's connection with Nyneve, who continues his role as protector and is herself (alongside Gareth) one of Malory's most positive characters, carries his authority by proxy into the future.

In each work discussed, the nature of Merlin's role parallels the religious concerns of the authors. Each author approaches the possibilities in a different way, using Merlin to comment--overtly, ironically, or implicitly--on the religious nature of his other characters and to develop the religious themes. In the HRB, Merlin's demonic background undercuts the blind faith of the British in him, and parallels their failure in Christian behavior. Their national character gives them a tendency to _superbia_, but God has not fated them to be as unrepentant as they are. He gives them a last chance under Arthur, but they fail to measure up. Geoffrey clarifies this British failing in the _Vita_ as he advances Merlin along his personal spiritual path, no partner in the national _superbia_. In the Vulgate, baptism saves Merlin from becoming the Antichrist and turns him toward preparing the British kingdom for its participation in the religious quest for the Grail. Merlin is not all-powerful, and he is part human, so his actions and his end both reflect his humanity (love) and his obedience to God's plan. The _Suite_ shows an even more human Merlin, whose more negative end reflects his passive resistance against his disappearance. His role here is more detached, more marvellous than in the Vulgate, reflecting the shift in religious emphasis from the communal to the individual. In Malory, then, the shift is even further, subordinating religion to politics. Although Arthur's actions definitely distance him from God, they also have profoundly negative effects on the kingdom and people he rules, and Malory's emphasis lies here. Religion, however, is an important aspect of society, one which can play both a spiritual (personal) and an ethical (social) role, and it plays a clear, but secondary, part in condemning Malory's Arthurian society.

Each work contains fantasy, but each uses it to different ends; as illustrated in the first chapter, both secular and religious works utilize this tool in furthering their particular ends. Just as marvels function for both "sides" in the story of St. Columba and the druids, so too in the fictional works. Merlin and Viviene, Morgain and Vortigern's clerks all display a certain mastery of the arcane arts, as do both Gwydion and Llwyd in the Mabinogi. Springs possess healing powers and people change shape at will. While fantasy may be one of the hallmarks of romance, it is clearly at work in other genres as well, and the perceptions of old which equated fantasy with children's (or second-rate) literature must be questioned. In connection with the prose romances, the marvels serve as reminders of the divine presence in the Arthurian world and underline the religious themes.

The varying degrees of "romance" which are seen in the two French works and in Malory parallel the extent and nature of Merlin's religious role. The Vulgate uses Merlin the most extensively, and in a very social context. The establishment of a firm regnal base on which the Grail story can be played out entails the building of a new society in Britain. Merlin's task is to ensure that that society is created and functioning, and that the steps along the Grail path are set in motion. The religious base is broad, encompassing all of that new society, realized symbolically by the united "crusaders'" defeat of the pagan hordes. Later in the cycle, the Quest becomes an intensely personal matter, but it grows out of the social base. The overwhelming "epicness" of the Vulgate

Merlin reflects this greater concern with the society rather than the individual.

The Grail foundation in the _Suite_ is somewhat different; although the background of Merlin remains the same and there is a clear connection between the Joseph era and Arthur's, the Dolorous Stroke intervenes and provides another reason for the Quest. The emphasis here is on personal religious and spriritual matters, with the social an outgrowth of the individual. Merlin's decreased role in the narrative and his character reflect the shift, as do the additional fantasy elements and the elimination of the extended warfare. This greater concern with the individual is a traditional romance plan of action.

As noted in the introduction, there is one further element in both of these works which acts to detour generic expectations: history (or what we now call legend). Both works are ultimately based on Geoffrey, and Geoffrey (for most medieval purposes) is history. Both works also bring in Robert's religious history. This double insistence on historical veracity is tied to Merlin. Merlin is found in Geoffrey prophesying the future; many medieval commentators took Geoffrey at his word and worked out detailed concordances for the prophecies--from history. Merlin is the devils' answer to Christ and his harrowing of Hell--also history. Merlin is the narrative authority, giving historical veracity to events both religious and secular. None of the "traditional" Arthurian romances is so emphatically tied to history, and none of them contains Merlin as a character. Indeed, "timelessness," and "the distant past" are the two phrases most often used in describing the settings of medieval romance, but Merlin rules out their use in the case of these works. All of the cycles, Malory included, frustrate traditional generic expectations.

The generic problem in connection with Malory is long-standing,[13] and the same things which frustrate Malory scholars apply to the French works; the French even have the additional problem of the greater religious connections. Some critics have thrown up their hands, with comments like, "It is doubtful whether the romance can be indeed regarded as a genre at all" (Gradon 269). Still, I believe it is possible to discover common ground, to find elements which are shared. No literary work is a faithful replica of another, and generic boundaries require fluidity and an ability to absorb otherwise alien matter. As the Arthurian prose cycles reveal, this fluidity can result both in discomfort (the absorption is often strained) and in a profoundly satisfying creation--the two are not mutually exclusive, though of course the most skilled authors will be able to avoid causing discomfort.

The Merlins created in the thirteenth century mirror both the faults and the virtues of the literary tradition. He can be many different things--divine messenger, king's advisor, buffoon, lover, devil--and these varied roles do not always fit well under one skin. All the same, he is as he is, a creature of his time and place, reflecting the concerns of his creators. While we may not always sympathize with their concerns, it behooves us to attempt to understand them correctly, or as best we can with our resources limited by temporal and cultural distance. I think T. H. White demonstrates that he understood well the underlying purposes to the thirteenth-century romances, as well as Malory, when he uses Merlin to express his twentieth-century concern over social and ethical conditions. While the sentiments are perhaps not shared, the reversion to Merlin as the ethical authority in Arthur's kingdom and his connection with the societal, historical theme are reflected in the magician's final lesson to the king:

> "In any case let us leave these dubious questions of politics to the dingy tyrants who look after them. Ten thousand years from now it may be time for the educated to concern themselves with such things, but meanwhile they must wait for the race to grow up. We for our part have offered a solution this evening to the special problem of force as an arbiter: the obvious platitude that war is due to national property, with the rider that it is stimulated by certain glands. Let us leave it at that for the present, in God's name." (*Book of Merlyn* 125)

Notes - Chapter Six

[1]These other Middle English works are: *Of Arthour and of Merlin* (ca. 1250-1300), an abridged verse translation up to Arthur's betrothal; Henry Lovelich's *Merlin* (ca. 1425), a verse translation of the first half of the Vulgate text; and a prose translation of the Vulgate *Merlin* (ca. 1450).

[2]Besides, this has been done rather satisfactorily by Ben F. Fiester in his 1966 dissertation on Malory's use of the supernatural; my arguments with Fiester mainly concern his comments on Malory's use of the French sources, about which Fiester seems to accept Vinaver's conclusions blindly while at the same time questioning Vinaver's conclusions about Malory. See *The Function of the Supernatural*.

[3]While I concur with Larry Benson's views (*Malory's Morte* 4) on the unity of Malory's narrative, it is nevertheless most convenient to continue to refer to the divisions in Vinaver's edition. References to Malory will be given in the text and are from *The Works of Sir Thomas Malory*, ed. Eugene Vinaver, 2nd ed. (three volumes with consecutive pagination).

[4]I concur here with Lumiansky, "Arthur's Final Companions" (10) and Fiester (7, 205).

[5]This comment, too, comes from a knight acquiescing in a plan to poison Arthur, which may indicate a bias on the knight's part.

[6]See Lumiansky, "Arthur's Final Companions" (16-19), Fiester (95-125), and Holbrook, "Nymue." All three comment on the good-evil opposition personified in these two women.

[7]Norris J. Lacy discusses the use of *contrappasso* as a principle of structure in Chrétien's romances, and the analogy seems equally appropriate here. See *The Craft of Chrétien de Troyes* 8.

[8]Benson, *Malory's Morte*, 32-33. Benson uses the Winchester ms. version, not Vinaver's, in his argument.

[9]See (among others) Brewer, "'The hoole book'"; Field, *Romance and Chronicle*; Allen, *The Ethical Poetic*, esp. 155-165; and Pochoda, *Arthurian Propaganda*.

[10]Jill Mann puts forward this argument in relation to the symbolic events involving Balin's sword in "'Taking the Adventure'" (78).

[11]My argument arises from the revision Pochoda makes on Moorman's idea that the knights' failure is due more to their lack of self-examination than a failure of their code. She argues that

an Arthurian knight is also "predisposed to fail by the inadequacy of his code" (27).

[12]She also notes the aggressiveness of the code loses its natural outlet when external enemies are overcome, thus resulting in increased internal struggles.

[13]Problems with classifying Malory are discussed in Vinaver, Allen, Field, Benson, and Pochoda. Pochoda even argues that, "Properly speaking there is no 'genre' to which we can assign the book" (69).

Appendix One - Robert de Boron's *Merlin*

Narrative Summary

Edition by Alexandre Micha, BN 747 (13th c.) base ms., supplemented by various others.

After Christ's harrowing of Hell, the devils plot to regain their control over men, deciding to create one of their own to do their will on earth. One demon is assigned to engender this instrument of their will; he first goes about destroying the family through a series of mishaps, leaving one of three daughters vulnerable to his plans. A holy man advises her on how to avoid the family's fate, and she succeeds until one of her fallen sisters intrudes upon her and causes her to forget in anger her ritual for one evening. This evening the demon has intercourse with her and engenders Merlin. The woman confesses at once to the holy man and the demons lose control over her. Because the child is baptized immediately, the devils also lose "their" child and their plans are for naught. Once the child is weaned, its mother is to be sentenced to death for her supposed sins.

From birth, Merlin is unusual for his hairy body and his precocious speech. At the age of two, he defends his mother before the judge, in the process revealing arcane knowledge about the judge's parentage. The woman's confessor, Blaise, examines Merlin thoroughly about his knowledge, concludes that the child is not a tool of devils, and becomes Merlin's protege.

Vortigern's betrayal of Constans and tyrannical rule are told, leading into the discovery of Merlin by the king's messengers. Merlin thrice reveals his arcane knowledge to the messengers and discredits the king's seers upon his arrival. The dragons beneath the tower are unearthed, and Merlin prophesies Vortigern's death. The sons of Constans land and begin to conquer their kingdom.

Once told of Merlin, Ambrosius and Uter send for him; Merlin meets the king's messengers in disguise, finally revealing himself to the king. Merlin amuses himself and the brothers with a further charade of shape-changing, ending with a promise to advise them. One baron prompts a triple-death prophecy from Merlin, which later is fulfilled. Merlin decides that subsequently all his prophecies will be obscure, so Ambrosius orders a record be kept of the prophecies.

Ambrosius is killed in battle against the Saxons, and Merlin transports the Giants' Dance from Ireland for the king's memorial. After hearing Merlin tell of the Grail and Joseph of Arimathea, Uter charges him to erect a third table in preparation for the quest. Soon Uter falls in love with Igerne and fights the duke. Merlin arrives to help Uter see Igerne in the castle, disguising the king, himself and Ulfin. The duke is meantime killed, and Uter marries Igerne after negotiating with her advisors.

Igerne reveals to Uter her pregnancy and her uncanny experience the night her husband was killed. She agrees to send the child away secretly, and Merlin arranges for its fostering. Years later, Saxons renew attacks, and Merlin helps Uter defeat them. Soon after, the king dies, and the barons consult Merlin regarding a successor. He suggests they reassemble at Christmas, which they do; at this time, the sword in the stone appears and Arthur is the only one who can draw it. Supported by the church and the commons, he becomes king. Several barons refuse to accept him.

[At this point, the manuscripts diverge. Micha completes Robert's text with Merlin arriving to reveal the king's parentage, the barons accepting the new king, and setting the scene for the Perceval-Quest.]

Appendix Two - *Lestoire de Merlin* (Vulgate)

Narrative Summary

Edition by H. Oskar Sommer, British Museum Add. Ms. 10292 (dated 1316).

After Merlin comes to court and reveals Arthur's heritage, eleven barons still refuse to acknowledge the king and rebel against him. The rebels are initially defeated with the help of Merlin, but manage to retreat. When Arthur holds court, Merlin advises him to send for Ban and Bors. The brothers arrive and, after receiving assurances from Merlin about the safety of their lands, agree to help Arthur. The combined forces rout the rebels; to add to the rebels' problems, news comes of Saxon invasions, which causes them to return strategically to their homes. Arthur and company (on Merlin's advice) move on to assist King Leodegan at Carmelide.

In Arthur's absence, his nephews, sons of some rebels, secretly leave home and take on the task of defending Logres against the Saxons for him. The youths are amazingly successful, though they do receive occasional (disguised) help from Merlin.

At Carmelide, the allies force the attacking King Rions to retreat. Leodegan learns who his rescuers are and fêtes them grandly. Action moves from Arthur, to Gawain and the other youths, to the rebel barons, and back to Arthur several times. Arthur and Gawain are successful, the rebels not, against the invaders. Merlin jumps between Logres and Carmelide as needed.

Merlin encounters Viviane and begins a series of visits to her in which he teaches her magic and falls in love. He also sets in motion Arthur's marriage to Leodegan's daughter, Guenevere, who brings as part of her dowry the round table and its knights which were once Uter's. Arthur returns to Logres, meets Gawain and his other defenders, and prepares for his wedding. In response to trouble in Gaul, Arthur and Gawain take their men to assist Ban and Bors and are successful.

From Gaul, Merlin goes on to Rome where he assumes several guises as the emperor learns of his unfaithful wife and faithful female (disguised) knight, Grisandole. After this episode, Merlin returns to Britain.

The wedding of Arthur and Guenevere nears, and the rebels plot to substitute the lady's look-alike half-sister on the wedding night. The plot, with Merlin's help, does not succeed, and the sister is banished. The rebel Lot then attacks Arthur, but is defeated by his own son, Gawain. Gawain reconciles Lot and Arthur.

Rivalry grows between two groups of Arthur's knights, known as the Queen's knights (Gawain and company) and the Round Table knights (who came from Leodegan). A tournament gets out of hand and the royal pair impose restrictions on fighting. Arthur's sister Morgain learns some magical skills from Merlin. Lot and his sons are sent on a mission to bring the rest of the rebels into Arthur's camp.

Encountering several groups of Saxons on the way, Lot's mission convinces the rebels to join with Arthur to drive the invaders out of Logres. The combined forces successfully defeat the various groups of Saxons established across the land. Ban engenders a son, Hector, with the help of Merlin's magic as the troops return to Camelot.

King Rions seeks revenge on Arthur, but is killed in the attempt. After this victory, Merlin goes to Jerusalem (disguised again), interprets a king's dream and is instrumental in converting him to Christianity. Merlin returns to Arthur's court, and on his heels arrives a beautiful lady accompanied by an ugly dwarf. The dwarf is knighted, and the two depart.

A message from Rome arrives, demanding that Arthur pay tribute, which he refuses to do. The armies set off for the continent; on the way, Arthur kills the giant of Mont St. Michel. The Romans are defeated. Arthur succeeds in freeing the Lausanne area of a vicious cat, then makes his way home. Merlin soon takes his final leave of Arthur and goes to Viviane who imprisons him.

Arthur, worried about Merlin, sends thirty men to seek the magician. The dwarf who was knighted earlier meets several of them, including Gawain. Gawain follows a voice and finds Merlin's prison, speaks with him, and sadly leaves the magician to his fate and returns to court. The volume ends with a brief recital of Ban's fate, introducing his son Lancelot, whose story is taken up in the next book.

Appendix Three - Suite du Merlin (Huth)

Narrative Summary

Edition by Jacob Ulrich and Gaston Paris, Huth ms. (British Museum Add. Ms. 38117) (late 13th/early 14th c.) supplemented by BN 747 to correct and fill lacunae.

[A few items are changed in the base: 1. the women with Merlin's mother attribute his abilities to God's presence rather than call him a devil; 2. Merlin discusses before the judge the nature of demonic and divine knowledge, that God had to give him the ability to see the future; 3. Constans' son is not taken out of the monastery by Vortigern, but succeeds to the throne as a boy and mismanages a Saxon invasion when Vortigern refuses to help out of pique.]

At the Pentecost court when Arthur is crowned, Lot's wife appears and the two, unaware of their relationship, have an affair. Arthur immediately is beset by dreams boding trouble for his land. While hunting the next day, he becomes separated from his men and encounters the marvellous Questing Beast and the knight who follows it, after which Merlin (disguised at first) arrives and reveals to Arthur the meaning of his dreams and his true identity.

Once back at court, Arthur sends for Ygerne (now alive, though mentioned dead earlier), who corroborates Merlin and Ulfin, and Arthur's parentage is now known. Adventures appear at court and knights are sent off on various missions, Merlin prophesying off and on about the future. Rather than retreating to Blaise in the wild,

Merlin suggests to Arthur that a record be made of his reign and sets many scribes to work at the task; Blaise joins the court circle.

Arthur rashly pursues an adventure, breaks his sword, and receives a new one with Merlin's help from an enchanted lake. The scabbard of this sword will protect its bearer from serious injury. Arthur tries to kill off the child who will destroy him, but does not succeed. The adventures of the knight Balin lead him eventually to transgress at the Grail castle and send a blight on the land. He and his brother mortally wound each other, and Merlin sets Balin's "dolorous" sword with a new hilt in an anvil to await Galahad.

In fighting against Rion, Arthur's men are victorious, but Lot is killed in the process and his sons swear vengeance on Pellinor, who killed Lot to save Arthur. Arthur entrusts his sword and scabbard to his sister Morgain, who makes a copy and gives the original, she thinks, to her lover to protect him. However, she provided the wrong one and this sets in motion her increasing enmity for her brother.

After Balin's adventures are complete, Arthur consults Merlin about choosing a queen, mentioning Leodegan's daughter. Merlin arranges this marriage; at the wedding feast Pellinor, Tor, and Gawain are each given an adventure to pursue as a lady huntress who appears at court following a white stag is carried off by a knight. This lady is Niviene, who, once rescued, stays at court among the queen's ladies, and Merlin falls in love with her.

Merlin teaches Niviene magic, but she fears him. When her father recalls her, Merlin accompanies her and they encounter a number of adventures. Merlin builds her an invisible manor by a lake. When Merlin sees Arthur in danger back in England, Niviene pushes him to return in spite of his foreboding about his end. After Merlin defeats two evil harper-enchanters, Niviene imprisons him in a lovers' tomb.

Morgain arranges a murder attempt on her brother by way of magic, but Niviene arrives in time to secretly thwart it; Arthur is now convinced of his sister's treachery and she flees. Her son, Yvain, is banished on her account, but his cousin Gawain elects to go with him. They encounter The Morholt and the three join together to go adventuring. They split up when three women, aged 15, 30 and 70, offer them adventures, agreeing to meet in a year.

The narrative ends with another attempt by Morgain to kill Arthur, through a magic mantle. In disguise, Niviene warns the king and he avoids death. She leaves, commending Arthur on his advancement of chivalry and expressing a wish that he continue to do so.

Works Consulted

I. Primary Sources

Adomnan's Life of Columba. Ed. A. O. Anderson and M. O. Anderson. London: Thomas Nelson, 1961.

Augustine of Hippo. _The City of God_. Trans. Henry Bettenson. Ed. David Knowles. Baltimore: Penguin, 1972.

"The Battle of Magh mucramha." _Silva Gadelica_. Ed. and trans. Standish H. O'Grady. 1892. NY: Lemma, 1970. 353-58.

Buched Dewi. Ed. D. Simon Evans. Cardiff: U of Wales P, 1959.

La Chanson de Roland. Ed. T. Atkinson Jenkins. 1929. With new bibliographical supplement. N.p.: American Life Fdn., 1977.

"De Chophur in da Muccida." _The Book of Leinster_. Vol. 5. Ed. R. I. Best and M. A. O'Brien. Dublin: DIAS, 1967. 1121-24.

Lestoire de Merlin. Ed. H. Oskar Sommer. _The Vulgate Version of the Arthurian Romances_, Vol 2. Washington: Carnegie Institution, 1908.

Geoffrey of Monmouth. _The Historia Regum Britanniae of Geoffrey of Monmouth_. Ed. Acton Griscom. London: Longmans, Green, 1929.

__________. _Historia Regum Britanniae: A Variant Version edited from manuscripts_. Ed. Jacob Hammer. Cambridge: Medieval Academy of America, 1951.

__________. _The History of the Kings of Britain_. Trans. with introduction by Lewis Thorpe. 1966. Baltimore: Penguin, 1982.

__________. _Vita Merlini_. Ed. Basil Clarke. Cardiff: U of Wales P, 1973.

L'Histoire de Guillaume le Maréchal. Ed. P. Meyer. 3 vols. Paris, 1891-1901.

Lancelot. Ed. Alexandre Micha. 7 vol. Geneva: Droz, 1978-1983.

Layamon. _Brut_. Ed. G. L. Brook and R. L. Leslie. Oxford: EETS, 1963, 1978.

Life of St. Declan of Ardmore and Life of St. Mochuda of Lismore. Ed. and trans. P. Power. Irish Texts Society 16. London: Irish Texts Soc., 1914.

"Life of St. Molasius of Devenish." *Silva Gadelica.* Ed. and trans. Standish H. O'Grady. 1892. NY: Lemma, 1970. 18-23.

Le Livre de Lancelot del Lake. Ed. H. Oskar Sommer. *The Vulgate Version of the Arthurian Romances,* Vols. 3-5. Washington: Carnegie Institution, 1908-16.

The Mabinogi and Other Welsh Tales. Trans. and ed. Patrick K. Ford. Berkeley: U of California P, 1977.

Malory, Sir Thomas. *The Works of Sir Thomas Malory.* 2nd ed. Ed. Eugene Vinaver. 3 vol. Oxford: Clarendon, 1967.

Merlin or the Early History of King Arthur. Ed. H. B. Wheatley. 3 vol. EETS os 10, 21, 36. London: EETS, 1865-69.

Merlin: Roman en prose du XIIIe siècle (Suite du Merlin). Ed. Jacob Ulrich and Gaston Paris. 2 vols. Paris, 1886.

La Mort le Roi Artu. Ed. Jean Frappier. Geneva: Droz, 1964.

Of Arthour and of Merlin. Ed. O. D. Macrae-Gibson. EETS 268. London: Oxford UP, 1973.

Pedeir Keinc y Mabinogi. Ed. Ifor Williams. 2nd. ed. Cardiff: U of Wales P, 1951.

Rhygyvarch. "Life of St. David." Ed. A. W. Wade-Evans. *Y Cymmrodor* 24 (1913): 1-73.

Robert de Boron. *Merlin.* Ed. Alexandre Micha. Geneva: Droz, 1978.

__________. *Le Roman de L'Estoire dou Graal.* Ed. William A. Nitze. Paris: Champion, 1971.

Le Roman de Balain: A Prose Romance of the Thirteenth Century. Ed. M. Dominica Legge. Manchester: Manchester U P, 1942.

Táin Bó Cúalnge from the Book of Leinster. Ed. Cecile O'Rahilly. Dublin: DIAS, 1967.

Vita Sancti Tathei *and* Buched Seint y Katrin. Ed. H. I. Bell. Bangor: Welsh Manuscripts Society, 1909.

Vitae Sanctorum Britanniae et Genealogiae. Ed. A. W. Wade-Evans. Cardiff: U of Wales P, 1944.

Vitae Sanctorum Hiberniae. Ed. Charles Plummer. 2 vol. 1910. Oxford: Clarendon, 1968.

Wace. _Le Roman de Brut_. Ed. Ivor Arnold. 2 vols. Paris: SATF, 1938, 1940.

White, T. H. _The Book of Merlyn_. Austin: U of Texas P, 1977.

II. Secondary Sources

Ackerman, Robert W. "Arthur's Wild Man Knight." _Romance Philology_ 9 (1955-56): 115-119.

__________. "Henry Lovelich's Merlin." PMLA 67 (1952): 473-484.

Adler, Alfred. "Problem of Aesthetic versus Historical Criticism in 'La Mort le Roi Artu.'" PMLA 65 (1950): 930-943.

Allen, Judson Boyce. _The Ethical Poetic of the Later Middle Ages: A Decorum of Convenient Distinction_. Toronto: U of Toronto P, 1982.

Altman, Charles F. "Two Types of Opposition and the Structure of Latin Saints' Lives." _Medievalia et Humanistica_ ns 6 (1975): 1-11.

Anwyl, E. _Celtic Religion in Pre-Christian Times_. London: Constable, 1906.

Apter, T. E. _Fantasy Literature: An Approach to Reality_. Bloomington: Indiana U P, 1982.

Attenborough, F. L., ed. and trans. _The Laws of the Earliest English Kings_. 1922. NY: Russell, 1963.

Beer, Gillian. _The Romance_. London: Methuen, 1970.

Benson, Larry D. _Malory's Morte Darthur_. Cambridge: Harvard U P, 1977.

Benton, John F. "Collaborative Approaches to Fantasy and Reality in the Literature of Champagne." _Court and Poet_. Ed. Glyn S. Burgess. ARCA 5. Liverpool: Francis Cairns, 1981. 43-57.

Bezzola, Reto R. "Der französich-englische Kulturkreis und die Erneuerung der europäischen Literatur im XII. Jahrhundert." _Zeitschrift für romanische Philologie_ 62 (1942): 1-18.

Bieler, Ludwig, ed. and trans. The Irish Penitentials. Scriptores Latini Hiberniae 5. Dublin: DIAS, 1963.

Blaess, Madeleine. "Predestination in some thirteenth-century prose romances." Currents of Thought in French Literature: Essays in Memory of G. T. Clapton. Ed. T.V. Benn, et al. Oxford: Blackwell, 1965. 3-19.

Bloch, R. Howard. Medieval French Literature and Law. Berkeley: U of California P, 1977.

Bloomfield, Morton W. "Episodic Motivation and Marvels in Epic and Romance." Essays and Explorations: Studies in Ideas, Language, and Literature. Cambridge: Harvard U P, 1970. 97-128.

________. "Symbolism in Medieval Literature." Modern Philology 56.2 (Nov. 1958): 73-81.

Bogdanow, Fanni, ed. La folie Lancelot. Beihefte zur Zeitschrift für romanische Philologie 109. Tübingen: Niemeyer, 1965.

Bogdanow, Fanni. "Morgain's Role in the Thirteenth Century French Prose Romances of the Arthurian Cycle." Medium Aevum 38 (1969): 123-133.

________. "Pellinor's Death in the Suite du Merlin and the Palamedes." Medium Aevum 29 (1960): 1-9.

________. "The Rebellion of the Kings in the Cambridge mss. of the Suite du Merlin." University of Texas Studies in English 34 (1955): 6-17.

________. The Romance of the Grail: A Study of the Structure and Genesis of a Thirteenth-Century Arthurian Prose Romance. Manchester: Manchester U P, 1966.

________. "The Treatment of the Lancelot-Guinevere Theme in the Prose Lancelot." Medium Aevum 41 (1972): 110-120.

Bollard, J. K. "The structure of the Four Branches of the Mabinogi." Transactions of the Hon. Society of Cymmrodorion for 1974-75 (1975): 250-76.

Booth, Wayne C. The Rhetoric of Fiction. Chicago: U of Chicago P, 1961.

Bowen, E. G. Saints, Seaways, and Settlements in the Celtic Lands. Cardiff: U of Wales P, 1969.

Brewer, Derek. "'The hoole book.'" Essays on Malory. Ed. J.A.W. Bennett. Oxford: Oxford U P, 1963. 41-63.

________. "Malory: The Traditional Writer and the Archaic Mind." Arthurian Literature I. Ed. Richard Barber. Suffolk: Brewer; Totowa: Rowman, 1981. 94-120.

Briel, Henri de, and Manuel Herrmann. King Arthur's Knights and the Myths of the Round Table: A New Approach to the French Lancelot in Prose. Collection le Roi Arthur #4. Paris: Klincksieck, 1972.

Bromwich, Rachel. "Celtic Dynastic Themes and the Breton Lays." Études Celtiques 9 (1960-61): 439-474.

________. "The Celtic Inheritance of Medieval Literature." Modern Language Quarterly 26 (1965): 203-27.

________. "The Character of the Early Welsh Tradition." Studies in Early British History. Ed. H. M. Chadwick, et al. Cambridge: Cambridge U P, 1954. 100-135.

________. "Concepts of Arthur." Studia Celtica 10-11 (1975-76): 163-81.

Brooke, Christopher. "Geoffrey of Monmouth as a Historian." Church and Government in the Middle Ages: Essays Presented to C.R. Cheney on His 70th Birthday. Ed. Christopher Brooke, et al. Cambridge: Cambridge U P, 1976. 77-91.

Brown, Peter. The Cult of the Saints: Its Rise and Function in Latin Christianity. Chicago: U of Chicago P, 1981.

________. "Sorcery, Demons and the Rise of Christianity: from Late Antiquity into the Middle Ages." Religion and Society in the Age of Saint Augustine. London: Faber and Faber, 1972. 119-146.

Bruce, James D. The Evolution of Arthurian Romance From the Beginnings down to the Year 1300. 2nd ed. 2 vols. Hesperia Erganzungsreiche 8. Göttingen: Vandenhoeck; Baltimore: Johns Hopkins P, 1928.

Bullock-Davies, Constance. "Exspectare Arthurum: Arthur and the Messianic Hope." Bwletin y Bwrdd Gwybodau Celtaidd 29.3 (Nov. 1981): 432-440.

Burns, Elizabeth D. Prison and Veil: The Structures of Image Patterns in the Arthurian Romances of the Vulgate Cycle. Diss. U of California, Berkeley, 1977. Ann Arbor: UMI, 1983. 7731306.

Burns, E. Jane. "Of Arthurian Bondage: Thematic Patterning in the Vulgate Romances." Medievalia et Humanistica ns 11 (1982): 165-76.

Caldwell, Robert A. "Wace's Roman de Brut and the Variant Version of Geoffrey of Monmouth's Historia Regum Britanniae." Speculum 31 (1956): 675-82.

Campbell, Joseph. "Mythological Themes in Creative Literature and Art." Myths, Dreams, and Religion. Ed. Joseph Campbell. NY: Dutton, 1970. 138-175.

Canary, Robert H. "Science Fiction as Fictive History." Many Futures, Many Worlds. Ed. Thomas D. Clareson. Kent, OH: Kent State U P, 1977. 164-181.

Carman, J. Neale. A Study of the Pseudo-Map Cycle of Arthurian Romances. Lawrence: U P of Kansas, 1973.

Chadwick, H. M., et al., eds. Studies in Early British History. Cambridge: Cambridge U P, 1954.

Chadwick, Nora K. The Celts. Baltimore: Penguin, 1970.

_________. "The Colonization of Brittany from Celtic Britain." Proceeding of the British Academy 51 (1965): 235-300.

_________, ed. Studies in the Early British Church. Cambridge: Cambridge U P, 1958.

Childress, Diana T. "Between Romance and Legend: 'Secular Hagiography' in Middle English Literature." Philological Quarterly 57 (1978): 311-322.

Clarke, Basil, ed. Vita Merlini. By Geoffrey of Monmouth. Cardiff: U of Wales P, 1973.

Clement, C. E. A Handbook of Christian Symbols and Stories of the Saints. 5th ed. Cambridge, 1895.

Cosman, Madeleine P. The Education of the Hero in Arthurian Romance. Chapel Hill: U of North Carolina P, 1966.

Crist, Larry S. "Les Livres de Merlin." Mélanges de langue et littérature françaises du moyen-âge offert à Pierre Jonin. Senefiance no. 7. Paris: Champion, 1979. 199-210.

Curley, Michael J. "A New Edition of John of Cornwall's Prophetia Merlini." Speculum 57 (1982): 217-249.

Delehaye, Hippolyte. The Legends of the Saints. 4th ed. Trans. Donald Attwater. New York: Fordham U P, 1962.

Eckhardt, Caroline D., ed. The Prophetia Merlini of Geoffrey of Monmouth: A Fifteenth-Century English Commentary. Speculum Anniversary Monographs 8. Cambridge: Medieval Academy of America, 1982.

Eliade, Mircea. Myth and Reality. 1963. NY: Harper Torchbooks, 1968.

Ellis, T. P. Welsh Tribal Law and Custom in the Middle Ages. Oxford: Clarendon, 1926.

Emmerson, Richard K. Antichrist in the Middle Ages. Seattle: U of Washington P, 1981.

Faral, Edmond. La légende Arthurienne. Paris: Champion, 1929.

Field, P. J. C. "Four Functions of Malory's Minor Characters." Medium Aevum 37 (1968): 37-45.

__________. Romance and Chronicle: A Study of Malory's Prose Style. Bloomington: Indiana U P, 1971.

Fiester, Ben F. The Function of the Supernatural in Malory's 'Morte Darthur'. Diss. Pennsylvania State U, 1966. Ann Arbor: UMI, 1983. 67-11,185.

Flint, Valerie. "The Historia Regum Britanniae of Geoffrey of Monmouth: Parody and Its Purpose--A Suggestion." Speculum 54 (1979): 447-468.

Ford, Patrick K. "The Death of Merlin in the Chronicle of Elis Gruffydd." Viator 7 (1976): 379-90.

__________, trans. and ed. The Mabinogi and Other Welsh Tales. Berkeley: U of California P, 1977.

__________. "The Poet as Cyfarwydd in Early Welsh Tradition." Studia Celtica 10-11 (1975-76): 152-162.

Fredericks, S. Casey. "Problems of Fantasy." Science Fiction Studies 14.5 (March 1978): 33-44.

Frye, Northrop. Anatomy of Criticism. Princeton: Princeton UP, 1957.

__________. The Secular Scripture. Cambridge: Harvard U P, 1976.

Gallais, Pierre. "La Variant Version de L'Historia Regum Britanniae et le Brut de Wace." Romania 87 (1966): 1-32.

Gantz, Jeffrey. "Thematic Structure in the Four Branches of the Mabinogi." Medium Aevum 47 (1978): 247-54.

Giffin, M. E. "A Reading of Robert de Boron." PMLA 80 (1965): 499-507.

Gradon, Pamela. Form and Style in Early English Literature. London: Methuen, 1971.

Greene, David. "Tabu in Early Irish Narrative." Medieval Narrative: A Symposium. Ed. Hans Bekker-Nielsen, et al. Odense: Odense U P, 1979. 9-19.

Griffin, Nathaniel E. "The Definition of Romance." PMLA 38 (1923): 50-70.

Grigsby, John L. "The Ontology of the Narrator in Medieval French Romance." The Nature of Medieval Narrative. Ed. Minnette Grunmann-Gaudet and Robin F. Jones. Lexington, KY: French Forum, 1980. 159-171.

Grosjean, P. "Life of St. Cadoc." An. Boll. 40 (1942): 35-67.

Gruffydd, W. J. Math fab Mathonwy. Cardiff: U of Wales P, 1928.

__________. Rhiannon: An Inquiry into the Origins of the First and Third Branches of the Mabinigi. Cardiff: U of Wales P, 1953.

Haas, Gerhard. "Struktur und Funktion der phantastischen Literatur." Wirkendes Wort, 28.5 (Sept.-Oct. 1978): 340-56.

Haidu, Peter. "Romance: Idealistic Genre or Historical Text?" The Craft of Fiction: Essays in Medieval Poetics. Ed. Leigh A. Arrathoon. Rochester, MI: Solaris, 1984. 1-46.

Hanning, Robert W. "The Social Significance of Twelfth-Century Chivalric Romance." Medievalia et Humanistica ns 3 (1972): 3-29.

__________. The Vision of History in Early Britain: From Gildas to Geoffrey of Monmouth. NY: Columbia U P, 1966.

Hartmann, Richard. La Quête et la Croisade: Villehardouin, Clari, et le Lancelot en prose. Boulder, CO: Postillion, 1977.

Heist, William W. "Irish Saints' Lives, Romance, and Cultural History." Medievalia et Humanistica ns 6 (1975): 25-40.

Hirsch, E. D., Jr. *Validity in Interpretation*. New Haven: Yale U P, 1967.

Holbrook, S. E. "Nymue, the Chief Lady of the Lake, in Malory's *Le Morte Darthur*." *Speculum* 53 (1978): 761-77.

Hyde, Douglas. "Medieval Accounts of Anti-Christ." *Medieval Studies in Memory of Gertrude Schoepperle Loomis*. Ed. Roger Sherman Loomis. Paris: Champion; NY: Columbia U P, 1927.

Ihle, Sandra Ness. *Malory's Grail Quest: Invention and Adaptation in Medieval Prose Romance*. Madison: U of Wisconsin P, 1983.

Jackson, Kenneth H. *The International Popular Tale and Early Welsh Tradition*. Cardiff: U of Wales P, 1961.

Jackson, Rosemary. *Fantasy: The Literature of Subversion*. London: Methuen, 1981.

Jameson, Fredric. "Magical Narratives: Romance as Genre." *New Literary History* 7 (1975-76): 135-63.

Jarman, A. O. H. "A Oedd Myrddin yn Fardd Hanesyddol?" *Studia Celtica* 10-11 (1975-76): 182-97.

__________. *The Legend of Merlin*. Cardiff: U of Wales P, 1970.

Jauss, Hans Robert. "Levels of Identification of Hero and Audience." *New Literary History* 5 (1973-74): 283-317.

__________. "Literary History as a Challenge to Literary Theory." *New Literary History* 2 (1970-71): 7-37.

Jones, Charles W. *Saints' Lives and Chronicles in Early England*. Ithaca: Cornell U P, 1947.

Jordan, Robert M. *Chaucer and the Shape of Creation: The Aesthetic Possibilities of Inorganic Structure*. Cambridge: Harvard U P, 1967.

Jung, Carl G. *Memories, Dreams, Reflections*. NY: Vintage, 1965.

Kagarlitski, Julius. "Realism and Fantasy." *SF: The Other Side of Realism*. Ed. Thomas D. Clareson. Bowling Green: Bowling Green U Popular Press, 1971. 29-52.

Kelly, F. Douglas. "L'Invention dans les romans en prose." *The Craft of Fiction: Essays in Medieval Poetics*. Ed. Leigh A. Arrathoon. Rochester, MI: Solaris, 1984. 119-142.

Kelly, Robert L. "Malory's 'Tale of Balin' Reconsidered." Speculum 54 (1979): 85-99.

Kennedy, Elspeth. "Merlin and the Role of Allusions in the First Part of the Prose Lancelot." BBSIA 12 (1960): 126-27.

_________. "The Role of the Supernatural in the First Part of the OF Prose Lancelot." Studies in Medieval Literature and Languages in Memory of Frederick Whitehead. Ed. W. Rothwell, et al. NY: Barnes; Manchester: Manchester U P, 1973. 173-84.

_________. "Social and Political Ideas in the French Prose Lancelot." Medium Aevum 26 (1957): 90-106.

Ker, W. P. Epic and Romance: Essays on Medieval Literature. 2nd ed. 1908. NY: Dover, 1957.

Kiessling, Nicolas. The Incubus in English Literature: Provenance and Progeny. Pullman: Washington State U P, 1977.

Kimball, Arthur Samuel. "Merlin's Miscreation and the Repetition Compulsion in Malory's Morte Darthur." Literature and Psychology 25 (1975): 27-33.

Knight, S. T. "Some Aspects of Structure in Medieval Literature." Parergon 16 (1976): 3-17.

Lacy, Norris J. The Craft of Chrétien de Troyes: An Essay on Narrative Art. Leiden: Brill, 1980.

_________. "The Form of the Brut's Arthurian Sequence." Jean Misrahi Memorial Volume. Ed. Hans R. Runte, et al. Columbia, SC: French Literature Publications, 1977. 150-57.

_________. "Spatial Form in Medieval Romance." Yale French Studies 51 (1974): 160-69.

Lagorio, Valerie. "The Apocalyptic Mode in the Vulgate Cycle of Arthurian Romance." Philological Quarterly 57.1 (Winter 1978): 1-22.

_________. "Joseph of Arimathea: the Vita of a Grail Saint." Zeitschrift für romanische Philologie 91 (1975): 54-68.

_________. "Pan-Brittonic Hagiography and the Arthurian Grail Cycle." Traditio 26 (1970): 29-61.

Lappert, Stephen F. "Malory's Treatment of the Legend of Arthur's Survival." Modern Language Quarterly 36 (1975): 354-68.

Leckie, E. William, Jr. _The Passage of Dominion: Geoffrey of Monmouth and the Periodization of Insular History in the Twelfth Century_. Toronto: U of Toronto P, 1981.

Lecouteux, Claude. "Introduction a l'étude du merveilleux médiéval." _Études Germaniques_ 36 (1981): 273-90.

Le Gentil, Pierre. "The Work of Robert de Boron and the _Didot Perceval_." R.S. Loomis, _ALMA_. 251-62.

Legge, M. Dominica. "Anglo-Norman Hagiography and the Romances." _Medievalia et Humanistica_ ns 6 (1975): 41-49.

_________. _Anglo-Norman Literature and Its Background_. Oxford: Clarendon P, 1963.

Lloyd, E. J. "The _Mabinogi_ as Literature." _The Celtic Review_ 7 (1911-12): 164-74, 220-48.

Loomis, Charles Grant. "King Arthur and the Saints." _Speculum_ 8 (1933): 478-82.

_________. _White Magic: An Introduction to the Folklore of Christian Legends_. Cambridge: Medieval Academy of America, 1948.

Loomis, Roger Sherman, ed. _Arthurian Literature in the Middle Ages: A Collaborative History_. Oxford: Clarendon P, 1959.

Loomis, Roger Sherman. _Celtic Myth and Arthurian Romance_. NY: Columbia U P, 1927.

_________. _The Development of Arthurian Romance_. 1963. NY: Norton, 1970.

Lot, Ferdinand. _Étude sur le_ Lancelot _en prose_. Bibliothèque de l'École des _Hautes Études_ no. 226. Paris: Champion, 1918.

Lot-Borodine, Myrrha. "Le double esprit et l'unité du _Lancelot en prose_." _Mélanges d'histoire du moyen âge offerts à Ferdinand Lot_. Paris: Champion, 1926.

Lumiansky, Robert M. "Arthur's Final Companions in Malory's _Morte Darthur_." _Tulane Studies in English_ 11 (1961): 5-19.

_________. "The Question of Unity in Malory's Morte Darthur." _Tulane Studies in English_ 5 (1955): 29-39.

Malinowski, Bronislaw. _Magic, Science, and Religion and Other Essays_. 1948. NY: Doubleday, 1954.

Manlove, C. N. "On the Nature of Fantasy." Schlobin 16-35.

Mann, Jill. "'Taking the Adventure': Malory and the Suite du Merlin," in _Aspects of Malory_. Ed. Takamiya Toshiyuki and Derek Brewer. Cambridge: Brewer, 1981. 71-91.

Marx, Jean P. "Persistance des traits celtiques de la figure de Merlin dans le roman arthurien." BBSIA 12 (1960): 124-25.

________. "Le sort de l'âme de Merlin mis en cause par l'évolution de son caractère." _Mélanges offerts à Rene Crozet à l'occasion de son 70. anniversaire_. Ed. P. Gallois and Y.-J. Rion. Poitiers: Société d'Etudes Médiévales, 1966. 981-83.

McKenna, Catherine A. "The Theme of Sovereignty in _Pwyll_." _Bwletin y Bwrdd Gwybodau Celtaidd_ 29.1 (Nov. 1980): 35-52.

Menard, Philippe. _Le Rire et le Sourire Dans le Roman Courtois en France au Moyen Âge (1150-1250)_. Geneva: Droz, 1969.

Micha, Alexandre. "La Composition de la Vulgate du Merlin." _Romania_ 74 (1953): 200-220.

________. _De la Chanson de Geste au Roman_. Publications romanes et françaises 139. Geneva: Droz, 1976.

________. _Étude sur le "Merlin" de Robert de Boron_. Geneva: Droz, 1980.

________. "L'Influence du _Merlin_ de Robert de Boron." _Mélanges d'Études Romanes du Moyen Âge et de la Renaissance offerts à M. Jean Rychner_. Travaux de Linguistique de Littérature 16.1. Strasbourg: Centre de Philologie et de Littératures romanes, 1978. 395-409.

________. "Les manuscrits du _Merlin_ en prose de Robert de Boron." _Romania_ 79 (1958): 78-94, 145-174.

Micha, Hugues. "Reflets du monde contemporain dans le 'Merlin' de Robert de Boron." _Revue des langues romanes_ 81 (1975-76): 395-430.

Miko, Stephen J. "Malory and the Chivalric Order." _Medium Aevum_ 35 (1966): 211-30.

Milburn, R. L. P. _Early Christian Interpretations of History_. NY: Harper, 1954.

Mobley, Jane. "Toward a Definition of Fantasy Fiction." _Extrapolation_ 15 (1973-74): 117-28.

Moorman, Charles. *The Book of Kyng Arthur: The Unity of Malory's Morte Darthur*. Lexington: U of Kentucky P, 1965.

Morris, Colin. *The Discovery of the Individual, 1050-1200*. NY: Harper, 1972.

Morris, Rosemary. *The Character of King Arthur in Medieval Literature*. Cambridge: Brewer; Totowa: Rowman, 1982.

Nelson, L. H. *Normans in South Wales 1070-1171*. Austin: U of Texas P, 1966.

O'Coileain, Sean. "A Thematic Study of the Tale *Pwyll Pendeuic Dyuet*." *Studia Celtica* 12-13 (1977-78): 78-82.

O'Driscoll, Robert, ed. *The Celtic Consciousness*. NY: Braziller, 1981.

O'Grady, Standish H., ed. and trans. *Silva Gadelica*. 1892. NY: Lemma, 1970.

Owen, Aneurin, ed. and trans. *Ancient Laws and Institutes of Wales*. 2 vols. London, 1841.

Pähler, Heinrich. *Strukturuntersuchungen zur* Historia Regum Britanniae *des Geoffrey of Monmouth*. Bonn: Rheinische Friedrich-Wilhelms-Universität, 1958.

Parry, John J. "Celtic Tradition and the *Vita Merlini*." *Philological Quarterly* 4 (1925): 193-207.

Paton, Lucy A. "Merlin and Ganieda." MLN 18 (1903): 163-69.

__________. "Notes on Merlin in the *Historia Regum Britanniae* of Geoffrey of Monmouth." *Modern Philology* 41 (1943): 88-95.

__________. *Studies in the Fairy Mythology of Arthurian Romance*. 2nd ed. NY: Burt Franklin, 1959.

__________, ed. *Les Prophécies de Merlin*. 2 vols. NY: Heath, 1926.

Patrides, C. A. *The Grand Design of God: The Literary Form of the Christian View of History*. London: Routledge, 1972.

Payen, J.-C. "L'art de récit dans le *Merlin* de Robert de Boron, le *Didot-Perceval* et le *Perlesvaus*." *Romance Philology* 17 (1963-64): 570-85.

Pelan, Margaret. *L'Influence du Brut de Wace sur les romanciers français de son temps*. Paris: Droz, 1931.

Peters, Edward. *The Magician, the Witch and the Law*. Philadelphia: U of Pennsylvania P, 1978.

Pfeiffer, Ruth. *En route vers l'au-dela arthurien. Étude sur les chateux enchantes et leur enchantements*. Zurich: Juris, 1970.

Philmus, Robert M. "Toderov's Theory of 'The Fantastic': The Pitfalls of Genre Criticism." *Mosaic* 13.3-4 (1980): 71-82.

Pickford, C. E. *L'Évolution du Roman Arthurian en Prose*. Paris: Nizet, 1959.

Piggott, Stuart. *The Druids*. NY: Praeger, 1968.

Plummer, Charles, ed. *Vitae Sanctorum Hiberniae*. 2 vols. 1910. Oxford: Clarendon, 1968.

Pochoda, Elizabeth. *Arthurian Propaganda: "Le Morte Darthur" as an Historical Ideal of Life*. Chapel Hill: U of N. Carolina P, 1971.

Poirion, Daniel. *Le Merveilleux dans la Littérature Française du Moyen Âge*. Paris: P U de France, 1982.

Powell, T. G. E. *The Celts*. London: Thames and Hudson, 1958.

Propp, Vladimir. *Morphology of the Folktale*. Trans. Laurence Scott. Ed. and rev. Louis A. Wagner. 2nd ed. Austin: U of Texas P, 1968.

Rabkin, Eric S. *The Fantastic in Literature*. Princeton: Princeton U P, 1976.

Rees, Alwyn, and Brynley Rees. *Celtic Heritage: Ancient Tradition in Ireland and Wales*. London: Thames and Hudson, 1961.

Ricardo-Gil, Joan N. *The Practice of Witchcraft and Magic in Fact and Fiction During the French Middle Ages*. Diss. Boston College, 1980. Ann Arbor: UMI, 1983. 8017616.

Roberts, Brynley F. "Geoffrey of Monmouth and Welsh Historical Tradition." *Nottingham Medieval Studies* 20 (1974): 29-40.

Robinson, Fred Norris. "Satirists and Enchanters in Early Irish Literature." *Studies in the History of Religions Presented to Crawford Howell Toy*. Ed. D. G. Lyon and C. F. Moore. NY: Macmillan, 1912. 95-130.

Rosenhaus, Myra Joan. *Britain Between Myth and Reality*. Diss. Indiana U, 1982.

de Rougemont, Denis. Love in the Western World. Rev. ed. 1956. NY: Fawcett, 1966.

Rubey, Daniel Robert. Literary Texts and Social Change: Relationships Between English and French Medieval Romances and Their Audiences. Diss. Indiana U, 1981. Ann Arbor: UMI, 1984. 8128044.

Rumble, Thomas C. "Malory's Balin and the Question of Unity in the Morte Darthur." Speculum 41 (1966): 68-85.

Ruff, Joseph R. "Malory's Gareth and Fifteenth-Century Chivalry." Chivalric Literature: Essays on Relations Between Literature and Life in the Later Middle Ages. Ed. Larry D. Benson and John Leyerle. Studies in Medieval Culture 14. Kalamazoo: Medieval Institute Publications, 1980. 101-116.

Russell, Jeffrey B. Dissent and Reform in the Early Middle Ages. Berkeley: U of California P, 1965.

__________. Witchcraft in the Middle Ages. Ithaca: Cornell U P, 1972.

Ryding, William W. Structure in Medieval Narrative. The Hague: Mouton, 1971.

Schlobin, Roger C., ed. The Aesthetics of Fantasy Literature and Art. Notre Dame: U of Notre Dame P, 1982.

Schmerl, Rudolf B. "Fantasy as Technique." SF: The Other Side of Realism. Ed. Thomas D. Clareson. Bowling Green: Bowling Green U Popular Press, 1971. 105-15.

Schneider, Marcel. La littérature fantastique en France. Paris: Fayard, 1964.

Scholes, Robert. Structural Fabulation. Notre Dame: U of Notre Dame P, 1975.

__________, and Robert Kellogg. The Nature of Narrative. London: Oxford U P, 1966.

Schwartz, Susan M. "The Founding and Self-Betrayal of Britain: An Augustinian Approach to Geoffrey of Monmouth's Historia Regum Britanniae." Medievalia et Humanistica ns 10 (1981): 33-53.

Smith, Patrick Coogan, ed. Les Enchantemanz de Breteigne: An Extract from a Thirteenth-Century Prose Romance "La Suite du Merlin". North Carolina Studies in the Romance Languages and Literatures 146. Chapel Hill: U N C Dept. Romance Languages, 1977.

Southern, R. W. _The Making of the Middle Ages_. New Haven: Yale U P, 1953.

Stevens, John. _Medieval Romance: Themes and Approaches_. NY: Norton, 1973.

Tatlock, J. S. P. "Certain Contemporaneous Matters in Geoffrey of Monmouth." _Speculum_ 6 (1931): 206-23.

_________. "Geoffrey of Monmouth's _Vita Merlini_." _Speculum_ 18 (1943): 265-87.

_________. _The Legendary History of Britain: Geoffrey of Monmouth's Historia Regum Britanniae and Its Early Vernacular Versions_. Berkeley: U of California P, 1950.

Thomas, Keith. _Religion and the Decline of Magic_. NY: Scribner's, 1971.

Thompson, Charles J. S. _Mysteries and Secrets of Magic_. London: John Lang, 1927.

Thompson, Raymond H. "Modern Fantasy and Medieval Romance: A Comparative Study." Schlobin 211-25.

Thorndike, Lynn. _The Place of Magic in the Intellectual History of Europe_. Studies in History, Economics and Public Law 24.1. NY: Columbia U P, 1905.

Thorpe, Lewis, ed. and trans. _The History of the Kings of Britain_. By Geoffrey of Monmouth. 1966. Baltimore: Penguin, 1982.

Toderov, Tzvetan. _The Fantastic_. Trans. Richard Howard. Ithaca: Cornell U P, 1975.

Tubach, Frederic C. "The Formation of the Miraculous as Narrative and Cultural Pattern: Remarks on the Religious Imagination of Gregory's Dialogues." _Deutsche Vierteljahrsschrift für Literaturwissenschaft und Geistesgeschichte_ 54.1 (1980): 1-13.

Vinaver, Eugene. "The Dolorous Stroke." _Medium Aevum_ 25 (1957): 175-80.

_________. _Form and Meaning in Medieval Romance_. Cambridge: Modern Humanities Research Assn., 1966.

_________. "La Genèse de la Suite de Merlin." _Mélanges de Philologie Romane et de Littérature Médiévale offerts à Ernest Hoepffner_. Paris: Les Belles Lettres, 1949. 295-300.

__________. "The Historical Method in the Study of Literature." The Future of the Modern Humanities. Ed. J. C. Laidlaw. Cambridge: Modern Humanities Research Assn., 1969. 86-105.

__________. Malory. 1929. Oxford: Clarendon, 1970.

__________. The Rise of Romance. NY: Oxford U P, 1971.

__________. "The Shaping Spirit in Medieval Verse and Prose." Sewanee Medieval Colloquium Occasional Papers 1 (Spring 1982): 9-18.

__________, ed. The Works of Sir Thomas Malory. 2nd ed. 3 vol. Oxford: Clarendon, 1967.

Wagner, Robert Leon. "Sorcier" et "magicien". Paris: Droz, 1939.

Walzel, D. L. "Sources of Medieval Demonology." Rice Univ. Studies 60.4 (Fall 1974): 83-99.

Watkin, Morgan. La Civilization Française Dans les Mabinogion. Paris: Didier, 1962.

Wehrli, Max. "Strukturprobleme des Mittelalterlichen Romans." Wirkendes Wort 10 (1960): 334-45.

Weiss, A. M. Merlin in German Literature. Catholic U of America Studies in German 3. Washington: Catholic U of America, 1933.

White, Hayden. "Fictions of Factual Representation." The Literature of Fact. Ed. A. Fletcher. NY: Columbia U P, 1976. 21-44.

Wilkin, Gregory. "'Benois Soit li Ieus': Points Taken and Mistaken in and on the Old French Vulgate Merlin." Court and Poet. Ed. Glyn S. Burgess. ARCA 5. Liverpool: Francis Cairns, 1981. 339-56.

Williams, Ifor, ed. Pedeir Keinc y Mabinogi. 2nd ed. Cardiff: U of Wales P, 1951.

Wilson, R. H. "The Cambridge Suite du Merlin Re-examined." Texas Studies in English 36 (1957): 41-51.

Wolfe, Gary K. "The Encounter with Fantasy." Schlobin 1-15.

__________. "The Known and the Unknown: Structure and Image in Science Fiction." Many Futures, Many Worlds. Ed. Thomas D. Clareson. Kent: Kent State U P, 1977. .

Wright, Thomas L. "On the Genesis of Malory's Gareth." *Speculum* 57 (1982): 569-82.

Zumthor, Paul. "La délivrance Merlin." *Zeitschrift für romanische Philologie* 62 (1942): 370-86.

__________. *Essai de Poétique Médiévale.* Paris: Seuil, 1980.

__________. "Merlin dans le Lancelot-Graal. Étude Thematique." *Romans du Graal au 12e et 13e siècles.* Strasbourg, 29 mars à 3 avril 1954. Paris: Mario Roques/CNRS, 1956. 149-164.

__________. *Merlin le Prophète.* 1943. Geneva: Slatkine Reprints, 1973.

For Product Safety Concerns and Information please contact our EU representative GPSR@taylorandfrancis.com
Taylor & Francis Verlag GmbH, Kaufingerstraße 24, 80331 München, Germany

www.ingramcontent.com/pod-product-compliance
Lightning Source LLC
Chambersburg PA
CBHW071411100726
47908CB00004B/1139

* 9 7 8 1 1 3 8 9 9 5 7 9 6 *